T0065404

Talking to the Dead

Talking to the Dead

AND OTHER STORIES

Sylvia Watanabe

Anchor Books
A DIVISION OF RANDOM HOUSE, INC.
NEW YORK

An Anchor Book
PUBLISHED BY DOUBLEDAY
a division of Bantam Doubleday Dell Publishing Group, Inc.
1540 Broadway, New York, New York 10036

Anchor Books, Doubleday, and the portrayal of an anchor
are trademarks of Doubleday, a division of Bantam Doubleday
Dell Publishing Group, Inc.

Talking to the Dead was originally published in hardcover by
Doubleday in 1992. The Anchor Books edition is
published by arrangement with Doubleday.

Book design by Guenet Abraham

Library of Congress Cataloging-in-Publication Data

Watanabe, Sylvia.
Talking to the dead and other stories / Sylvia Watanabe.
p.   cm.
1. Hawaii—Fiction.   I. Title.
[PS3573.A799T3   1993]
813'.54—dc20   93-18336
CIP

ISBN 978-0-385-41888-1

FIRST ANCHOR BOOKS EDITION: AUGUST 1993

145052501

*For my mother, Betty Chiyoko Watanabe, and
for my father, Walter Hiroshi Watanabe,
with love*

ACKNOWLEDGMENTS

Warmest thanks to William Osborn, Carol and Joseph Bruchac, Heidi Von Schreiner, and my editor Sallye Leventhal, who have made possible what has so often seemed improbable.

CONTENTS

Talking to the Dead

Anchorage

The needle glinted in my grandmother's hand as she appliquéd Bird Tracks onto a square of white cotton. She glanced from Father, dozing in his lawn chair, to Aunt Pearlie with her head buried in the *County News*, to me, then began, "Last night I dreamed . . ."

Little Grandma was always having dreams. She said the spirits of our kin watched from the shrine on her bedroom dresser and spoke to her while she was sleeping. She said they told her when to go down to the beach to harvest seaweed, and where to look when Cousin Makoto misplaced his store teeth, and what chicken to bet on at the chicken fights.

"In my dream, it was dark," she said. "There was no sun, no moon, no speck of light in the whole sky. Then a hole opened somewhere on the other side of the darkness, and it opened, and opened, and opened . . ."

"I think we get the picture." Aunt Pearlie yawned.

Father snored softly, his mouth slightly open as if in surprise.

It was a hot summer afternoon, and we were cooling off under the poinciana tree in Little Grandma's front yard. I had just graduated from the university and was visiting home a few weeks before leaving for Anchorage and my first real job as an art teacher in a public high school. I had never been away from the islands before, and was caught between the anticipation of a new, independent life and the sensation of being cast adrift, with everything familiar slipping further and further away. I shivered as I smoothed the blank page of the sketchpad lying open on my lap, and Little Grandma reached over to squeeze my hand.

"Would you look at this." Aunt Pearlie gestured at the item she'd been reading. The headline said, "Rise in Peeping Tom Incidents." Before I could read further, she folded the paper away, then declared, "But it doesn't surprise me one bit, considering the depraved goings-on right here under our very noses."

If there was anyone who'd given much consideration to that particular subject, it was my aunt Pearlie. Among the members of the Buddhist Mission's Ladies Auxiliary, she took an especially keen interest in the moral, and immoral, affairs of the community. Each morning, after seeing her husband Freddy Woo off to the sugar mill and putting her house in order, she set out for Little Grandma's. There, strategically positioned at the top of the lane overlooking the rest of the village, she carried out her surveillance work from the front yard.

"Why, just the other day," she continued now, "Emiko McAllister was telling me that the Laundry Burglar is on the loose again. What do you suppose Someone Like That would want with our clean wash?"

"All it takes is a bit of imagination," Little Grandma said. "Now, Hana, where was I?"

I fidgeted with the wire binding on my sketchbook but didn't answer. Aunt Pearlie scowled.

"Hana, do you remember?" Little Grandma repeated.

"Oh, Mama," Aunt Pearlie almost shouted. "Something about a hole in the sky, for Pete's sake. Besides, if it was as dark as you say, how did you even know where the sky was?"

"Because I was *standing up,*" Little Grandma said. "And as I stood there, the sky opened and opened . . ."

Aunt Pearlie rolled her eyes.

". . . and colors came pouring out of it," Little Grandma went on, "until there were colors where there'd only been darkness before."

"Then what?" I asked.

"Then I woke up."

"What?" Aunt Pearlie said. "What kind of a dream is that?"

Little Grandma smiled, and continued to stitch at her appliqué.

Down the hill, the cloud shadows drifted over the sugar fields. The shifting green and yellow of the cane, the red furrows of earth, and the blue curve of the water joined into a patchwork of shapes and colors. On the opposite shore of the bay, the skyline bristled with the metal and glass towers of the fast-spreading resort town, where there had been miles of empty beach and some of the best net fishing on the island just ten years before. I remembered accompanying my father when he'd gone there to sketch the Hawaiian fishermen, and how they'd taught us to identify the schools of fish, flashing beneath the surface of the water. Green for *manini*. Silver for *papio*.

Now, as I removed the cover from my box of oil crayons, I became aware of him watching me. He had wakened from his nap and was sitting up in his chair. His gaze shifted away from my face and moved out across the fields, then back to the box of colors on my lap. "That," he whispered, pointing to one of them. I held the box toward him, and he picked out black.

Later that afternoon, I left my grandmother and aunt disagreeing over what to cook for supper, and slipped off to my father's studio above the garage. "How many kinds of black can you see?" I remembered him asking as I learned to mix paints. His luminous, unfinished canvases gathered dust along the walls. In the sunny corner where he'd once worked, his easel still looked toward the window; a brush tipped with vermilion lay across the square of Plexiglas he'd used as a palette. Among the pencil drawings and color studies tacked to the wall were fliers for juried exhibits he'd planned to enter.

After my mother's death, when I was about a year old, Father and I had come to live with Little Grandma in Luhi, where he'd grown up. For the next seventeen years, he'd worked on the maintenance crew at the sugar mill and spent all his spare time painting. Then, just after I left for college in Honolulu, the "forgetting sickness," as Little Grandma called it, had begun creeping up on him. The first sign of anything seriously wrong occurred during a routine repair at the mill, when he took apart a piece of machinery and was not able to put it back together again. Soon afterward, my grandmother reported to me that he'd quit his job and had begun spending all his time in his studio. When I returned for the winter holidays, a few weeks later, I found him sitting at his easel, applying layer after layer of black to a single spot in the middle of the canvas. That was just before he'd stopped painting altogether.

Now, though he often seemed lucid, it was hard to tell what still had the power to reach him. He needed help dressing and feeding himself, and rarely spoke. As I wandered through his studio, I remembered the hours I had spent there as a child, coloring at the old table which we'd rescued from a neighbor's trash and which was now cluttered with dried-up tubes of pigment and dusty pages of yellowing newsprint. It was at that table that he'd given me my first "seeing lessons."

"Look, Hana," I could still hear him saying. "Everything is made of light."

"It's a pity, isn't it?" The sound of Aunt Pearlie's voice startled me.

I made an agreeing noise, then said, "The place sure could use a good going-over. Just look at this dust."

"If the dust was all we had to worry about, we wouldn't have a problem. We need to make plans," she said.

I knew that she wanted to discuss my father's future, a subject we'd been skirting ever since my return. I turned to face her. "What's that you got there?" I asked, pointing to her bulging shopping bag. "Smells like fish with black bean sauce."

Aunt Pearlie snapped, "Your uncle Fred's got to eat, poor man. And don't think I don't know what you and your grandmother are up to—always changing the subject when we need to get some serious talking done."

I said, "If you mean about Father, that's up to Little Grandma, isn't it? In fact, she tells me that he's gotten much better these last few months, since she's begun taking him to the Prayer Lady." The Prayer Lady was famous in all the villages around Luhi for her healing touch.

"Your papa needs more than a good massage to fix what's wrong with him," Aunt Pearlie retorted. "And as for whose business it is, who do you suppose Mother turns to when you're not around?"

After she left, I went downstairs to help Little Grandma with Father's dinner, but she was already taking care of it. She murmured to him as she proffered spoonfuls of rice and fish, which he accepted passively, his eyes fixed blankly ahead. "Where are you now, Koshiro?" she said.

I couldn't help thinking that my aunt had been right. He was getting worse. I pushed the thought away and went to join Little Grandma at the kitchen table. "Here, let me do that," I said.

"We're nearly finished," she answered, without taking her eyes off my father. "But we'll be heading upstairs for a bath pretty soon. Would you mind bringing in the clean towels?"

"If the Laundry Burglar hasn't already gotten to them," I said.

Little Grandma looked at me then. "Ah, poor Pearlie," she said, but she was smiling.

That night I dreamed of the snow. The dream never changed. In it, I was crossing a vast, wintry field with no trees, or landmarks, or colors for as far as I could see in any direction. With each step, I sank further into the deep, white drifts—first to my ankles, then to my knees, and finally up to my hips. As I struggled to get free, it quietly began to snow.

I woke, as usual, with my heart racing. For a moment I imagined I was already in Alaska, until I began recognizing familiar objects in the room around me. The mahogany toy cabinet with the china tea set sitting on top, the red wooden child's rocker, and on the far wall the mural my father painted the year I turned six. Here and there in the moonlight, I could make out a tangerine-colored bear, a flying dog, a rabbit in top hat and tails.

The sound of Father's snoring came from his bedroom down the hall, and I thought of how he had been when he'd made those paintings. "Come Hana!" I could hear him calling, as I drifted back into sleep. "Oh, Hana, come see!" And once again, I was running toward his voice. When I arrived, he pointed to a crown flower hedge alive with monarch butterflies.

"Akai tori, ko tori," Little Grandma was singing upstairs in the attic. "Red bird, little red bird, why are you so red?" As she paused for breath, I could hear the crisp sound of her sewing shears, cutting patchwork.

· · ·

"We'll all be in a nursing home before she finishes that thing," Aunt Pearlie said. "She's been working at that same quilt for the past hundred years, I'd swear."

It was the following afternoon, and she and I were sitting at the kitchen table looking out the window at Little Grandma and Father in their usual spot under the poinciana. Aunt Pearlie had appeared at the kitchen door before lunch, determined to corner me into a chat. For the past half hour she'd been trying to convince me that Father required professional care.

"I don't like it," I objected. "We can't just pass him on to a bunch of strangers. Besides, Little Grandma would never agree."

She said, "Look, Hana, nobody *likes* making this sort of a decision, but we don't have a choice. You've seen what a handful he can be—even when you're around to help."

The morning light flickered across the walls, and the contours of the room shifted, as the boundaries between shapes melted and colors slid away into shadow.

"If Mama were by herself," Aunt Pearlie went on, "she could sell this place and come stay with me. You know the Canadian investment company that built the new hotel across the bay? Well, one of their representatives dropped by about a week ago. He told me they wanted to buy some land around here to put up a time-sharing condominium."

As I was processing this information, the front gate squeaked open. It was Emi McAllister from down the road. She was carrying what looked like a dish or tray in a brown grocery bag.

"What's she got there?" Aunt Pearlie reached for the spectacles in her apron pocket and put them on. "Hmmm. Probably some of that brown fudge that sticks to the roof of your mouth. Or a bunch of those hard little puffed rice cakes."

Emi stopped to talk to Little Grandma, then came inside and handed her parcel to my aunt.

"Oh, rice cakes," Aunt Pearlie said, opening the bag and withdrawing a dish of the confections.

"Just a little welcome home for Hana." Emi smiled at me. "Your papa's looking fine."

"Well, he's not fine," Aunt Pearlie said and offered her the cakes.

Emi waved them aside. "Never touch the stuff, too hard on my old teeth." She patted my hand. "Things going badly, huh?"

Aunt Pearlie frowned. "So, Emi, how're you doing? What's the latest on the Laundry Burglar?"

"Mrs. Koyama says the Dancing School Teacher is missing her white satin nightcap," Emi answered. "Everyone knows that woman wears a wig."

Aunt Pearlie said, "It's disgraceful that this situation has been allowed to go on for so long."

"You have to admit, he hasn't done much of anything in the last four or five years," Emi said.

"Still, you never know what a twisted mind like that will think up next," my aunt pointed out. "Today he steals our laundry, tomorrow he murders us in our beds. I say it's about time the police began doing their jobs."

Emi said, "From what I hear, the sheriff doesn't have much to go on. The burglaries always stop before any real clues turn up."

"Meantime, you don't know how I worry," Aunt Pearlie said. "I can't be here with Mother twenty-four hours a day. And Hana will be leaving for Anchorage soon."

"That's odd," Emi said. She was looking out the window.

"It's more than odd," Aunt Pearlie replied.

Emi motioned toward the front yard. "I was just talking to your mother out there a minute ago."

The quilting mat was still spread out under the tree, but the wind had blown the cover off a box full of patchwork, leaving a trail of Bird Tracks across the yard. Neither Father nor Little Grandma was anywhere to be seen.

While Aunt Pearlie and Emi went to check with the neighbors, Little Grandma came limping up the road to the house. She had been concentrating on a tricky place in her sewing when Father took the opportunity to slip away.

After Aunt Pearlie returned and got on the phone to the police, I decided to go and check the beach. I remembered that, after the resort began going up across the bay, Father had confined his sketching excursions to the rocky coastline around Luhi. Every weekend in fine weather, he'd take his paintbox and portable easel out onto the lava jetty that enclosed our side of the water. Sometimes I'd go with him, especially in winter, when there were whales about, and he and I would compete to spot the beautiful plumes of spray rising above the waves.

"Father!" I called now, scanning the rocks and tidal pools along the shore. The sky and sea were the color of fire. A wave broke over the lava shelf and came swirling around my ankles. I had to hurry; the tide was rising.

Then I saw a speck of white out on the point. I picked my way across the jagged rocks, the waves crashing higher and higher, until I was wading through knee-deep water.

"You've scared us all to death," I scolded as I pulled myself up beside him.

He turned toward me, his face transfixed. He gestured toward the glittering path of red and gold, leading from where he stood, across the water, to the sun. "Look, Hana," he said.

"I just turned my back for one second," Little Grandma was explaining downstairs in the kitchen as I drew the water for my father's bath.

"That's all it takes," I heard Aunt Pearlie reply.

Father sat shivering on the edge of the tub, watching me.

"Just a minute and I'll help you out of those wet things," I said.

He had not spoken since I found him out on the point. "Father, you've got to say something." I unbuttoned his shirt and helped him pull his arms through the sleeves. "If you don't say anything, people will think they can do anything they want to you." I got his undershirt over his head, then kneeled before him and began unlacing his shoes. I looked into his face. "Father, talk to me. I heard you out there."

The sound of quarreling came up the stairs. "Hard-headed old woman!" Aunt Pearlie shouted. There were heavy footsteps across the living room, and the front door slammed.

My father reached for the gold chain around my neck. "Talk to me," I whispered.

.   .   .

The next morning I was wakened by the noise of my grandmother's antique washing machine rocking back and forth on the cement patio. The smell of burning french toast filled the room. I went downstairs to the kitchen and turned off the stove, then poured myself a cup of the tepid brown liquid from the aluminum coffeepot next to the sink.

As I took my first sip, Aunt Pearlie came in from hanging the wash. She said, "That's for the plants. Didn't you see the grounds at the bottom?"

I shook my head and pushed my cup away.

She came over and sat next to me, then began clasping and unclasping her hands as she stared out the window. Finally, she spoke again. "That was quite an adventure yesterday."

"Mmm. Do you know where Little Grandma is?" I asked.

"She and your father have gone off to the Prayer Lady's," Aunt Pearlie said.

I got up and went to fill the kettle. "Maybe I *will* have some of that bottled stuff."

Aunt Pearlie said, "Hana, we keep going around and around about this and not getting anywhere, but the Laniloa home isn't at all what you think. It's brand new, and well run, and Clyde Sakamoto—you know, of Sakamoto Hardware—says that his mother-in-law gets the best of treatment there. The least you could do is drive over and take a look."

"That won't be necessary," I said, "because I'm not going to Anchorage. I've decided to stay here and help Little Grandma take care of Father."

She was silent. Her hands lay very still upon the table. Then she drew something silky and white from her apron

pocket. I thought at first that it was a piece of fancy lingerie, and I wondered what my practical-minded aunt
would be doing with such a thing. As she smoothed it flat
on the table between us, I saw that it wasn't lingerie at all
but some sort of hat, trimmed with lace.

Aunt Pearlie's mouth was set in a stubborn line. "And
will you also take care of this?" she said. "I found it in one
of your father's pockets."

I had no idea what she was getting at, until I looked
out the screen door at the laundry hanging in the backyard,
and it struck me.

"I believe this nightcap belongs to the Dancing School
Teacher," she said.

Aunt Pearlie threatened to hand Father over to the law if
Little Grandma and I didn't agree to put him into the
home. "I'm only thinking about what's best for all of us,"
she said before going off to spend the rest of the afternoon
at Emi McAllister's.

As we watched her striding away down the road, Little
Grandma said, "Heaven spare us from Pearlie's worst."

We were sitting out under the poinciana. Overhead, the
sunlight glimmered through the canopy of red flowers,
casting a warm glow across the blank sketchpad lying open
on my lap. "Maybe I'll be able to draw when I get to
Alaska," I said, and felt the tears begin to come. "I can't go
to Alaska."

Little Grandma put aside the square she'd been stitch-
ing and took my face in her hands. "Of course you must
go," she said. "It won't make a bit of difference if you stay,
but it will make all the difference in the world if you
don't." A sly smile flickered across her lips. She woke my

father, then gestured at me to follow them toward the house.

She led us up the stairs to her room on the second floor. Inside, it was nearly bare—except for a tiny cot with a hard loaf-shaped pillow, the family shrine on the cedar dresser, and a calendar from Rusty Chan's Automotive Repair. She directed us through the narrow door leading up the rickety flight of stairs to the attic.

The room was well lighted from windows covering the walls on two sides, and it had been cleared of all the clutter that one usually finds in attics. Instead, there were trunks spilling over with bolts of new fabric, and cardboard boxes stuffed with articles of clothing. I could make out one of Father's old painting smocks, a floral shift of Aunt Pearlie's, and my first party dress. In the middle of the floor lay a mat surrounded by brown paper bags and shoe boxes filled with piecing in various stages of completion. Among the patterns I recognized were Ocean Waves, Hands All Around, Delectable Mountains, and Mongoose in the Pigeon Coop.

A rusty fan stood next to a quilting frame in a nearby corner. On the frame was a half-finished quilt of interlocking circles in seven colors, each standing for one of the jewels in Buddhist teaching. "I call that my Seven Treasures," Little Grandma said.

But it was to the far end of the room that my eyes were drawn. There hung an immense quilt, bordered by squares of bright-colored Bird Tracks. Though unfinished, the quilt covered nearly the entire wall. From where I stood, perhaps fifteen feet away, it seemed to contain every color in the entire world.

I moved closer, and the colors began to cohere into squares, the squares into scenes—each scene depicting

places and people in the life of the village. There were the
sugar fields sloping down to the water. The green and
white company houses with a different-colored dog in every yard. The singing tree. The old head priest leading the
procession of lights toward the sea. There was Henry
Hanabusa performing his nightly calisthenics, and Emi
McAllister in her garden. Every detail had been carefully
chosen—down to the green and pink scarf on her tiny sun
hat.

I looked closer. There was something familiar about the
fabrics from which the pieces of appliqué had been cut. My
heart quickened as I glanced at the last scene, of Aunt
Pearlie hanging the wash. It was pinned but had not yet
been stitched.

"I had to improvise on that one," Little Grandma said.
"I was all set to do Minerva Sato's tap-dancing comeback,
but Pearlie discovered the nightcap before I could make use
of it. So I decided to do one of her instead. Pinned it just a
little while ago."

"Were you and Father in this together?" I asked.

"It started by accident," Little Grandma explained. "He
ran off one day, and when I brought him home, I found his
pockets full of someone else's laundry. I was too embar-
rassed to return it, but I couldn't throw it away. Then I got
the idea of making this quilt, and began going out with
him." She watched to see how I was reacting, then added,
"I made sure we took only very small items."

"As if that made any difference," I said. "It's because of
your pilfering that we have to put Father away."

"No, Hana, it's Koshiro's illness that's stealing him
from us," Little Grandma said.

I went to stand next to my father, who was looking out
one of the windows. From where we were, we could see

into the yards of all the houses around us. Across the road, the vacant lot where I had played as a child was up for sale, and it was rumored that a fried chicken operation from Texas was interested in setting up a franchise there. At the far end of the village, I could see the gleaming new structure of the Laniloa Geriatric Care Facility and, below it, the boats anchored in the harbor. Beyond the harbor stretched the open sea.

I looked at my father and his lips were moving. I leaned close to catch his words. He was saying, "To not forget."

Emiko's Garden

Mr. Ah Sing, the Vegetable Man, told the Koyama Store Lady that Doc McAllister had finally gone *pupule* as they watched him come out his front gate at quarter to six on Saturday morning. Dressed in Day-Glo orange shorts, a kelly-green T-shirt, and a yellow baseball cap, McAllister paused on the sidewalk in front of his house to perform a few sets of calisthenics before setting off.

"That crazy old man is pushing fifty already," Mrs. Koyama observed. "Where's he going that he has to run?"

"Looks like he's aiming to reach a hundred." The Vegetable Man laughed and continued unloading his truck. His

arms moved rhythmically, balancing the weight of the pro-
duce crates.

"*Ai ya.*" Mrs. Koyama laughed too. "He'd get there
faster if he stayed home and slept."

Emi McAllister turned in an embrace of half sleep toward
the sound of her husband's footsteps disappearing up the
road. Without opening her eyes, she drew the warm sheets
close and pressed her face against his pillow. The morning
smelled of lavender from the garden, and rain.

As she lay drowsing, she thought of how familiar she'd
become with all the different views of McAllister's backside
—driving off in the middle of the night to deliver babies,
walking away toward waiting airplanes, retreating out the
back door to avoid her anger, paddling after the perfect
wave on the rolling back of the sea. He had taken up
running two years before, on his forty-fifth birthday, when
he'd decided that he was going to live forever.

McAllister's mother claimed that anyone who ran that
much couldn't be up to any good; she was suspicious of an
excess of anything, except orneriness, which she described
as "character." Emi wasn't entirely inclined to disagree. But
whether McAllister was in retreat or pursuit, she'd never
decided; it all seemed part of his singular struggle to attain
what he'd once called a kind of grace—moments lived so
intensely that all of one's passion and skill were brought to
bear on them.

McAllister splashed through rain puddles up the center of
the village, past the giant mesquite on fire with bougainvil-
lea. Past the Buddhist temple and the Paradise Mortuary.

He snatched a glimpse at himself in the window of the Sakamoto Hardware; YOU'RE NOT GETTING OLDER, the cigarette ad behind his reflection said.

It was coming easily now. The sleep was gone from his limbs, and the old stiffness in his right calf had worked itself out. The salt air felt good on his face and neck. He remembered the girl. Her hands, her bold yes-look, her black hair spilling upon the sand. His blood sang. Five miles out. Five miles back. He'd run his fastest mile his last year in college during the Regionals. There'd been a lap and a half to go, and Joey O'Day was in first; he was in second. He kept pushing the pace, but O'Day wouldn't break. Then they were in the final stretch, and McAllister passed him. The crowd was yelling.

"Cockadoodledoo!" McAllister's mother shouted out her bedroom window. She'd been wakened by the crowing of the fighting cocks, as McAllister ran past the Filipino camp.

Emi got out of bed and hurried down the hall.

"Get up! Get up!" the old woman yelled.

"Hush, Mother," Emi said, coming into the room. "You'll wake the Tamayoshis." Mr. Tamayoshi, the Japanese schoolmaster, lived with his spinster daughter in the cottage next door. But Emi was too late. The lights were already blazing in their windows. She could hear bewildered voices calling to each other. "Are you all right?" "What's happened?"

"Mack! Mack mack mack!" Sammy Lee's ducks joined in from several backyards away.

· · ·

The light was changing quickly now as the sun rose, burning away the rain. McAllister wiped his eyes with the back of his hand and struggled upward against the hill. His chest burned.

"Slowpoke!" He remembered how the girl had called from the raft, her hair flowing over her brown shoulders. She'd dangled her legs in the water, sending sparks of sunlight rippling across the surface. Just as he'd been about to reach her, she'd risen and plunged, laughing, into the sea.

McAllister crested the top of the hill and began to descend the other side. He resisted the flow at first, as he always did, until he was sure. "Come," she said, pulling him down. He yielded to the downward slope, and it was easy again. Her arms around him, her warmth like a gift.

When Emi got home from handing out apologies and rice cakes to the neighbors, she gave her mother-in-law a dish of mountain apples and settled her in a lawn chair within sight of the garden. It was nearing seven, but McAllister wouldn't be back for another half hour.

She walked down the gravel path between the herb bushes, stopping now and again to scoop up a handful of soil or to pinch off a leaf and turn it over in her hand. She noted the mint sprawling toward the marjoram beds and the new siege of caterpillars attacking the basil. She pulled out the carrots her mother-in-law had planted under the allspice, the tomatoes in the potted laurel, the cucumbers among the sage. "Why don't you grow some real vegetables?" the old woman always chided her.

Emi stopped to weed under the lavender. The herb

breathed its scent into the air, reminding her of photographs in gilded frames and camphorwood trunks filled
with handmade lace, like she'd seen at the Parmeter Estate
where she worked on the housekeeping staff years before.
She dug deeper, and the fragrance rose from the damp
ground and clung to her hands, her skin, her clothes. She
went deeper still into the clayey subsoil where the roots of
the plant reached tenaciously down. Under the mango tree,
the old woman was singing. Emi thought of fresh-scrubbed
young women in white linen dresses. She thought of the
girl. . . .

. . . It had just been one of those things, McAllister decided all over again, as he turned onto the coast road leading back to the village. He smiled. A sense of well-being
spread through him. Two miles to go. Underfoot, the puddles were beginning to evaporate, and the road felt familiar
and sure. The sky was luminous with sun. . . .

. . . as it had been that morning, when Emi had driven his
mother to the new shopping center across the bay. On their
way through the mall, they'd passed a young Filipino evan-
gelist with pomaded hair and a green and orange plaid
jacket, shouting in the middle of the plaza. "Brothers and
sisters, He is waiting with open arms!" His shouts echoed
off the concrete walls. Emi had turned to hush her mother-
in-law, who was beginning to mutter about people making
spectacles of themselves in public places, when she
glimpsed McAllister in the crowd.

. . .

"Hey, Doc!" Freddy Woo called from across the road. He was polishing his powder-blue Cadillac out on the parking strip in front of his house.

McAllister slowed and came over. He asked, "How's it going—the back okay?"

"Not bad. But now I get headaches," Freddy answered. He glanced at Haru Hanabusa watering the chrysanthemums in her yard next door, then leaned over and whispered, "My neighbors give them to me."

The two men laughed, and McAllister started on his way again.

His back had been to her, but Emi recognized the tilt of his head, the attentive, listening stance. She knew if she'd looked a little harder she could not have missed the girl. She no longer heard the preacher's shouting; she'd felt only the huge, prying hunger to *see*.

McAllister had moved away from the crowd, still bent toward his companion. Was he putting his arm around her? Emi had moved to follow. Suddenly, she'd become aware of his mother tugging at her sleeve. "What are you looking at?" the old woman demanded. "What do you see?"

Emi closed her eyes and breathed in. "Nothing," she said, willing the trembling in her voice to stop. "Nothing." She repeated the word firmly, then turned and placed herself, deliberately, in the old woman's line of vision. "I was looking for that new sushi place Mrs. Koyama is always talking about."

"But I saw you looking *at* something," her mother-in-law persisted.

"I think the restaurant's in that direction," Emi continued, without looking back. "They have all kinds of good things—yellowfin, squid, salmon roe . . ."

Her mother-in-law's face had lighted up, and she'd said, "I don't suppose they'd have some steak tartare?"

Now, McAllister's mother sang. Emi made one last thrust at the soil, then pulled. The lavender came out of the ground with a tearing sound. She laid down her trowel and went into the house to put on the coffee.

McAllister approached from the opposite direction than he'd set out. Already, the sun seemed too hot, and he was glad for the newly installed air conditioning in his office. He thought of hot coffee, slices of cold papaya, and biscuits melting with butter, then looked at his watch to make sure he had time to eat before getting to work.

When he arrived home, he greeted his mother, who was digging in the garden, then went around to the back of the house and called, "What's for breakfast?"

Emi was at the kitchen door, waiting. Her cotton frock had been bleached white in places by the sun and did not conceal the gentle sagging of her flesh beneath. As he climbed the steps toward her, he could smell the lavender on her skin.

"You running fool," she said, but her voice was soft. "Hurry and change out of those wet things before you catch your death of cold."

The Caves of Okinawa

Promptly at a quarter to six, the opening bars of a Sousa march, punctuated by spirited counting, began to issue from the house of the retired night watchman. Henry Hanabusa had commenced his evening calisthenics.

One, two. The temple bell rang, as the strains of "Semper Fidelis" soared over the mock orange hedge through open windows down the road.

Three, four. Henry's neighbor Freddy Woo looked up from the screen of his brand-new secondhand TV and frowned.

Five, six. Lulu Amalu slipped into her best going-out

dress, then stepped to the window to watch for the six o'clock bus from the city to pass.

Seven, eight. Mrs. Hundred Cats called to her cats. And all the village wives bade good night to each other over backyard fences and went to feed chickens, bath fires, children, and the ghosts of their dead kin.

"*Namuamidabutsu*," Henry's wife Haru chanted, summoning the hungry ghosts to eat. Everything was in its place: the candles lit, the incense burning, the offering dishes filled with rice. "I'll feed you forever, but keep us safe.

"Keep us safe from the cat girl's ghost, the evil eye, peeping toms, biting dogs, kidnappers, cancer, hippie fiends, laundry thieves, and the Twenty-one Great Afflictions, including fire, flood, and ungrateful children . . ."

The list took nearly ten minutes to recite from beginning to end. She kept it all down in a little notebook which she referred to from time to time, but no matter how many things she could think of to be kept safe from, there was always something more. Some things you could hardly find the words to say, like what happened to that old man in Arkansas who fell backward into a garbage can on his porch and died, days later, still wedged tight.

People were always getting into trouble over things they couldn't name. "Keep us safe from getting stuck," Haru prayed.

Lately, during the six months since her son Jimmy had been sent to Vietnam, she had taken to supplementing her regular keep-us-safes with a hundred extra *namuamidas* every day and weekly offerings of sweet rice cakes and oranges at the temple down the road. When she suggested to Henry that he might help with an occasional prayer or temple offering, he'd said the only thing that could help their boy now was a couple of thousand in hard cash and a one-way ticket to Canada. Afterward, Haru could not help thinking that such a blatant lack of faith would surely be noted by the ancestral spirits, and might possibly undo the benefit of her own good works. So, every night when she cooked supper, she'd been slipping excerpts from the Diamond Sutra, written on tiny strips of rice paper, into her husband's food.

Already, her diligence had begun to pay—just as it had when she'd chanted Henry himself through the Invasion of Okinawa. In those days, he'd been engaged to Flora, her younger sister. But Flora had been worse than no help at all. After she was diagnosed with that blood disease all she did was lie in bed all day and listen to love songs on the Victrola and cry.

Haru studied the portrait that was sitting in front of the altar—the wispy hair, fragile bones, and watery, dark eyes. She remembered how Flora had looked, lying in her coffin, her delicate fingers curled like a sleeping child's. Flora would not be a fierce ghost; she would be a lingerer, hanging about deserted graveyards and lovers' lanes. She'd passed on before the bonds of wedlock could cure her hankering for romance.

Haru withdrew her son's most recent letter from her apron pocket and sighed. It was a hankering for romance that had gotten Jimmy into all that Lulu trouble a couple of years back, when he nearly flunked out of school for playing hooky. Haru had found out too late for prayers to do him any good. Otherwise, he might be in college now, like his cousin Fat Billy Ing, studying to be a tax lawyer instead of getting shot at in Vietnam. She closed her eyes and breathed in the strange, musty scent that lingered on the folded pages. "Bring him back safe," she whispered to the photographs of her mother and father that flanked her sister's picture. Today her boy was coming home.

"Don't go discouraging him with a lot of gloomy memories," Haru had been reminding Henry every five minutes since they'd found out about Jimmy's leave. "Don't ask how things are going over there unless he brings it up first. Don't say, 'Back in my time, I remember, In the old days, Did you ever hear . . .' "

Henry finished the last of his sit-ups and got to his feet as the "Colonel Bogey March" came to an end. *"Namuamidabunamuamidabunamidabuabudabudabudabu,"* he could hear Haru chanting from down the hall. After restarting the record and debating for a second between push-ups and jumping jacks, he went to his desk and retrieved the bottle of Gilbey's that he kept stashed there. The best thing about a regular exercise routine, he decided as he uncapped the bottle and settled back with his feet on his desk, was that he could time it to coincide with his wife's evening devotions. Her chanting depressed him, the way its mournful cadences persisted in the mind for hours after.

During the war he'd even imagined the sound of it following him to Okinawa. Sometimes, in the stillness of the caves, he would hear her voice echoing down the lava corridors in the dark. The voice of doom, Flora had called it in her letters to him. Henry tilted his bottle, wiped his mouth with the back of his hand, and sighed, as the warmth of the liquor spread through his chest. In her letters, Flora had never given the slightest hint of how sick she was. He frowned, trying to call up her face and remembering small hands, a slender neck, a smooth curve of cool dark hair. Where her face should have been, there was a blank, like a spot on an old photograph faded to white. But there were other memories from that time that had not faded away, the ghosts of Okinawa that began to haunt him again when his son was called overseas.

Still, as Haru was always pointing out, what would an old man know about new wars? The kids nowadays were out marching in the streets because they knew better than to go. In the old days, the army had to turn boys away from the recruiting lines—all the Chinese, Filipinos, and Okinawans trying to prove they weren't Japs, and all the Japs trying to prove they weren't the ones who'd bombed Pearl Harbor. After Henry and his best friend Tag Asato were turned down by the 442, they'd enlisted as translators for Military Intelligence. They went for eight months of training in Minnesota, then were assigned to the Allied Translator Interpreter Service and sent to Okinawa.

Before they signed on, they'd imagined themselves in the thick of the action, translating secret documents or interrogating enemy generals. Instead, they were attached to one of the Australian cleanup crews that moved into an area when the fighting was over. They were called cave flushers. It had been their job to go into the tunnels among the cliffs and persuade the remnants of the Japanese Imperial Army, and the local villagers who'd fled with them, into surrendering.

Once more, Henry recalled how it had been, crawling into the opening of a cave and calling into the darkness. From somewhere inside, he'd hear whispered conversations, an old man's cough, a mother comforting a sobbing child, while out in the sunlight overhead, Corporal Jack Beasley and his men scrambled among the rocks, wiring them with dynamite. Sometimes the occupants refused to hand themselves over. Then, with all of them still inside, he and Tag would help seal the entrances, and the gunnery sergeant would order the charges fired.

The job had been especially hard on Tag, whose folks were from the Ryukyus. "Be sure and look up old Uncle Kinichi," they'd told him before he shipped out. "Give our best to Aunty Nobuko." A few months after their unit arrived in Okinawa, Tag saw his father's village burned to the ground and the drowned bodies of his father's family decomposing on a rocky beach. Henry had never forgotten the stench that hung on the wet, salt air. "Did the Japanese do this?" he'd asked a white-bearded grandfather, one of the few survivors. The old man told him how the villagers had panicked when they heard the Allies were coming. After setting fire to their houses, many had climbed up onto the cliffs and thrown themselves into the sea.

For the rest of their tour, Tag had seemed to be holding himself together. Then, a week after they returned home to Luhi, his mother went out to the bath shed and found him lying next to the drain on the cement floor, with a straight razor in one hand and both his wrists slit open.

Henry lifted his bottle for another swallow, then breathed out sharply as the liquor burned down his throat. Lately, he couldn't look at a paper or sit through the war news on TV without thinking about Jimmy and wondering if Vietnam was going to get his boy the way Okinawa had gotten Tag.

Suddenly, he became aware of the television booming the six o'clock news from Freddy Woo's living room next door. When he got up to pull the window shut, he could see his neighbor standing outside in his boxer shorts, with the sliding doors to his living room pulled open behind him. Freddy sipped the beer he was holding, then grinned and waved. Suddenly infuriated, Henry walked over to the phonograph next to his desk and turned up the volume. Then he went and yelled out the window, "What's the matter, you cheap *paké,* can't get any sound out of that piece of junk?"

Freddy retreated through his sliding doors, then reappeared looking grim, as his television blared out the latest casualty statistics from his living room. Henry responded with a rousing blast of the "Colonel Bogey March." By this time Freddy's wife Pearlie had come out and was shouting something at him. A group of neighbor ladies had begun to congregate in the Cat Lady's front yard across the road. For a minute Freddy held his ground and stood impassively sipping his beer; then he turned and disappeared inside his house. A few moments later, he came staggering out with an enormous mahogany television console in his arms. After setting it down on the porch, he stood leaning against it for a while, panting hard. When he recovered, he reached down with a flourish and turned up the sound as far as it would go. Not to be outdone, Henry rushed over to his phonograph, pulled the plug, and began dragging the speakers over to the window. Suddenly there was a muffled explosion from Freddy's porch, then silence. A buzzing rose from across the road, and a chorus of female voices shouted threats to call the law. When Henry got back to the window, the neighbor ladies were beginning to disperse, and Pearlie was shooting the smoking television set with a fire extinguisher. Downstairs, someone was banging at his front door.

"It might interest you to know," Haru said, coming into the room, "that Freddy Woo is outside yelling that you owe him a new television set."

"Crazy Chinaman blew it up himself. You saw him."

"I didn't see a thing, except two old fools carrying on like they'd lost what little sense they had in the first place." She sniffed, then narrowed her eyes. "What's that you got there? You been drinking again?"

Henry tucked the bottle of liquor behind one of the speakers, which were now sitting on the bookcase next to the window, then pointed outside. "It might interest *you* to know that there's a crazy man tearing up your flower beds," he said.

By the time Haru got to the window, Freddy had ripped out the last of the chrysanthemums in the front yard and was stalking off toward his house. "You did this on purpose, didn't you, Henry?" she said, facing him. "Tonight of all nights, you just had to do it."

As she turned to leave the room, Henry plugged in the phonograph, then positioned the needle at the beginning of the first track. The "Stars and Stripes Forever" poured from the speakers. "Nine hundred ninety-nine thousand, nine hundred ninety-nine, one million!" he yelled as the door closed behind her.

The kitchen was filled with a metallic odor, as if one of the electric burners had been left on high, but there was no smell of cooking food. Haru went to the oven and peered inside; she was trying something new the butcher had told her about. A meatless meatloaf, he'd called it, made out of reconstituted soybeans. She could hear it sizzling beneath its covering of aluminum foil.

Haru thought about how she had tidied the flower beds that morning. They were ruined now, with the mums about to bloom. If that wasn't just like Henry, undoing in a second what she'd struggled months to put together. When their son was growing up and she was trying to save his teeth, there was Henry stuffing the child with sodas and ice cream. She couldn't bake a cake without Henry slamming the door and making it fall, or have friends over to dinner without him getting the husbands so drunk, none of the wives would speak to her afterward for weeks.

Then there was the time after he'd mustered out when he went on a three-day bender that ended with him driving his pickup through the picture window of Doc McAllister's surgery. It was Haru who'd taken two weeks of her hard-earned pay and bailed him out of jail. It was she who'd rocked him through the nights when the war ghosts called him by name and liquor wouldn't shut out the sound of their voices. But even as she'd lain with the full weight of him on her, it was Flora he cried to. Flora, who was no more than a ghost herself, dying in her hospital bed. Can't you hear them, Florrie, he cried out, they're calling me back to the caves. If Haru had had any sense, she would have let him go then, let those dead Okinawan villagers have him for good.

Haru went from window to window, drawing the curtains. She would worry about the flower beds in the morning; she would let Henry deal with Freddy Woo. The evening shadows settled around her, cozy and comforting. She surveyed her tidy kitchen for something to put right, then pinched a dead leaf from the pot of geraniums on the sill and straightened the spice canisters next to the sink. As she reached into the cupboard to take the dishes down for supper, she paused, listening.

From outside came the rumble of an engine up the road. The bus from the city had rounded the corner; now it was wheezing to a stop, just out in front. After it roared away, she could hear the front gate opening and footsteps on the walk. Then Henry was bursting through the kitchen, yelling, "Come on, old woman, let's get some light on the subject." Next thing, he was out on the porch, and there were those greeting sounds men make, thumping each other on the back. Haru tried to follow, but her legs wouldn't hold her. "Where's Ma?" she heard her Jimmy say. He pushed open the screen door and came inside. "Hey, Ma," he called. "What're you doing here in the dark?" But all she could do was put her face in her hands and stand there shaking. She was glad, so glad she couldn't look.

"Back in my time . . ." Henry began, as he and Jimmy sat at the dinner table, sipping beers. Haru gave him a warning look, then began setting out dishes of grated raw carrots, icicle radish, and head cabbage in front of him.

"Health food," she said over her shoulder to Jimmy as she headed down the hall to the kitchen. "It's good for heart attacks."

"And unfit for human consumption," Henry added, but she was already out of earshot.

Jimmy turned to his father. "You been having more trouble with your heart?"

"Not a damn thing wrong with my ticker," Henry protested. "Besides, if I ever started having pains, I'd just go into my study over there and do a half dozen push-ups and that would fix me up as good as new."

Jimmy laughed, then said, "I see Ma's still got you on that exercise routine." He twisted around in his chair and surveyed the room—the plastic-covered furniture, the lace doilies under the table lamps, the china dog bookends sitting side by side on top of the breakfront cabinet. "You can't say she doesn't keep things in hand. Everything's exactly the same as when I left."

"Yeah, nothing much changes around here," Henry agreed. "But how are things going over there for you?"

Before the boy could answer, Haru was back with a tossed salad and a large, rare steak which she set down in front of him. "Eat while it's still hot," she urged, then turned and walked back in the direction of the kitchen. She returned in a moment with a gray, cheesy-looking substance in a Pyrex loaf pan. "And this is for us," she said, placing the pan in front of Henry.

"What is it?" he demanded. The gray cheese was covered with gray sliced mushrooms.

"It's a tofu mushroom loaf," she said.

Henry plunged the serving spoon into the loaf and scooped out a helping which promptly disintegrated into half a dozen pieces. "How come *he* gets a real steak?" he asked, pointing at Jimmy.

"Active boys need red meat," Haru answered.

Jimmy cut his steak in half. "Here, Pop, do you want some?"

"No, no, he really mustn't," Haru said. She spooned a bit more of the tofu loaf onto Henry's plate, then served herself and took a mouthful. "Hmmm, not bad at all," she said, but her voice lacked real conviction. She turned brightly toward her son. "So what are your plans now that you're home? Have you been keeping in touch with any of the old gang?"

"Some of them," Jimmy answered.

"Heard anything from that Lulu Amalu?" she asked.

"What is this, Twenty Questions?" Henry broke in. He poked at his food. "And what are these white things in here? How come everything you feed me these days is filled with these white things?"

"I don't know what you're talking about," Haru said, without taking her eyes off their son.

Henry peered at the contents of his dish. "It's paper," he said. His tone was accusing. "You've been feeding me paper."

"Don't be ridiculous," Haru said.

Henry picked a tiny scrap of confetti out of his meatless meat and held up his fork. "What do you call this?" he demanded. "The damned thing's got writing on it."

Haru said, "There's no need to raise your voice."

"I'll raise my voice if I damn well please," Henry yelled, then threw down his fork and started across the room.

"Where do you think you're going?" she asked.

"To get something to eat," he growled, and slammed out the door.

Haru said, "The way that old man carries on, you'd think I was the one who told him to go and get a heart attack."

Jimmy put down his knife and fork. "Look, Ma," he offered, "why don't I try to bring him back?"

"You stay where you are and finish eating. Your father will be all right." She reached for his hand, but he pulled away gently and got to his feet.

"I'm going after Pop," he said. Before she could say another word, he was out of the house and up the walk.

· · ·

Henry had just made it past Freddy Woo's and was slowing to a more leisurely pace when Jimmy caught him. "Wait up," he called. "Where're you headed?"

"Just up the road a bit," Henry replied. "Smell that?" The aroma of fresh-cooked food emanated from the houses around them. He sniffed in an appreciative way as they passed each one. "Teriyaki chicken," he said. "Fried shrimp. *Lau Lau.*" Jimmy paused at the corner to look at the apartment where Lulu lived, above her grandmother's store.

"Someone expecting you?" Henry asked.

"Could be," Jimmy said, then grinned.

After they'd passed the houses, Henry turned off into the gravel drive of Rusty Chan's Automotive Repair and went around to the back where the cars were parked. He stopped next to a '49 DeSoto sedan, then pulled his keys out of his pocket and began searching for one to fit the lock.

"What a beaut," Jimmy said, and gave an admiring whistle. "What's it doing here?"

"Freddy Woo was letting it go cheap a few months ago, so I bought it off him. But the thing never ran right, and just last week it stalled on the road out here. When I went to Woo, he refused to give my money back. Serves him right his TV blew up."

Jimmy had gotten the hood open and was looking inside. "Aren't you going to try and get it fixed?"

"Sooner or later," Henry said. "When Rusty gets around to it. In the meantime, I come out here whenever I need some peace and quiet." He unlocked the back door on the driver's side, then stepped inside and switched on the light. In front, where the seats had been was a small bookshelf stocked with Louis Lamour cowboy novels and a cooler filled with canned drinks. The back seat was covered with an old chenille bedspread and a couple of greasy-looking cushions. All of the windows had pulled-down shades.

"Hey, Pop, great pad," Jimmy said. "Who's your decorator?"

Henry looked up from rummaging around inside the cooler. "You like it? I've been thinking about going into business."

Jimmy came around to the passenger's side and leaned in through the window. He asked, "You notice any steam coming out of the engine before it stalled?"

"It used to make a terrible racket when you tried to start it, and you couldn't drive any distance before it would overheat. Could be a hole in one of the hoses," Henry said. "How about a drink? I've got NeHi, Primo beer, sloe gin, Spruce Knob white. Nothing cold, though. I forgot to bring ice."

Jimmy waved his offer aside. "It could be a hose—or even the belt to the water pump. Think Rusty would mind if I returned tomorrow for a better look?"

"Help yourself," Henry said. He opened a warm Primo, then reached into the glove compartment and pulled out a bag of pink and green shrimp chips. He offered the bag to Jimmy, who declined. "That's right. You had steak." Henry took a sip of beer. "But you never told me how things are going with you."

Jimmy stood up and stretched. Then he turned and stared off over the hills where the last fingers of sunlight were streaking the sky. "I don't know," he finally said. "Pretty good—if you consider they haven't got me yet. Not so good—considering I'm always scared shitless." He took out a cigarette and lit it.

Henry sipped his beer, then asked, "Did I ever tell you about my friend Tag Asato?"

Jimmy said, "You mean the guy who wasted himself?"

"Yeah, that was him," Henry said. "Anyway, when we were in Okinawa, Tag used to say, 'We're not gonna be here forever. I can take it as long as it's not forever.' He never figured that some things keep on going when they're supposed to be over." Henry reached up and grasped his son's arm. "Tag didn't have a choice, so maybe things couldn't have turned out any different for him. But nowadays a person has *options*."

Jimmy took a drag on his cigarette and exhaled it slowly out of the side of his mouth. He didn't take his eyes from his father's face. "So what are you getting at?"

Henry winked. "You tell me," he said.

"Isn't that just like a man, making a mess and leaving a woman to clean it up," Pearlie Woo said the next morning as she watched Haru turning the soil in her flower beds.

"What mess?" Haru asked. She removed her gardening gloves and wiped her forehead with the back of her hand. "You call this a mess? The way I look at it, Freddy was doing me a favor. You wouldn't believe how sick of those chrysanthemums I was getting."

"Well, I wasn't exactly referring to Freddy," Pearlie replied. "You can't deny it was Henry who started this whole thing."

Haru threw her hoe into a wheelbarrow full of crab grass and plant clippings, then said, "What Henry does is on his own account." But she couldn't help glancing at the television set, which was now sitting on the Woos' front porch.

Pearlie looked at the set too and shook her head. "It hasn't been a week since I brought that thing home from the flea market. It weighed a ton and we had to pay the Vegetable Man to haul it back. I thought it would keep Freddy home at nights." She paused meaningfully. "But after yesterday's little to-do, he went off to the La Hula Rhumba Bar and didn't get in till past one this morning."

"Pearlie, I'm very sorry about your television," Haru said. "But Henry is the person you should be talking to." She tilted the wheelbarrow up and began pushing it along the side of the house, toward the compost bin in the back-yard.

"Hold on a minute," Pearlie said as she hurried to keep up. "You haven't heard the best part yet. I didn't tell you who Freddy saw there."

Haru kept going.

"It was your boy," Pearlie called after her. "And he was with that Lulu Amalu."

Haru emptied the contents of the wheelbarrow, then headed for the back door. Imagine the nerve of that old gossip. It was amazing her tongue didn't shrivel up and drop right out of her head. You couldn't trust that busy-body Pearlie farther than you could throw her; and yet, Haru had to admit, there had been something suspicious about Jimmy's behavior the night before.

After letting herself into the house, she went straight to her son's bedroom and knocked at the door, but there was no answer. Henry was running the water in the bathroom down the hall. She knocked again, then turned the handle and went inside. Jimmy's suitcase sat unpacked on the stool next to the dresser. The sheets on the bed seemed as fresh as when she had put them on the previous afternoon.

Henry had come out of the bathroom and was rummaging around in the kitchen. When she got there, he was sitting at the table with his eyes closed and an ice pack on his head.

"Did Jimmy come in with you?" she asked. "I went to wake him just now, and he wasn't there."

Henry groaned and opened his eyes. "I don't even know when *I* came in—much less how, or with who. So put a lid on it."

"I tell you, his bed hasn't been slept in," Haru insisted.

"You don't know that," Henry pointed out. "In the army, that's the way they train you to make a bed."

Haru dumped an orange onto the cutting board and whacked it in half, then squeezed the juice into a glass. She said, "I know what I saw, and I saw that that boy's bed hasn't been slept in."

Behind her, Jimmy came bounding up the back porch steps into the kitchen. He kissed her on the cheek and handed her a bag of fresh-picked guavas.

She scowled. "Where have you been?"

"I got up early and went for a walk," he said, then turned to his father. "On the way back, I dropped by to look at the car, and I'm almost sure it's the belt to the water pump." He made everything look so easy, standing there lying, with the sunlight pouring all over him.

During the next week, Haru continued to keep an eye on Jimmy, the little she saw of him, during dinner. "I don't think I've spent two minutes with that boy since he's been home," she grumbled to Henry. "What does he thinks this is, some kind of a free restaurant?" But Henry said that was an error no one in their right mind was likely to make.

Each day her vigil began the minute she woke, when she padded down the hall and peeked in on Jimmy's room. But after that first morning he never failed to be there. Then, while he was out, she went through his shirts—checking for lipstick stains and the telltale scent of ladies' cologne. She even added several items to her list of keep us safes, all having to do with the wiles of women. And just in case Jimmy came in and might be listening, she made sure to give special emphasis to that part of her prayers. Nevertheless, much as she did not want to believe the worst, if the worst meant that Jimmy had once again succumbed to the dubious charms of Lulu Amalu, Haru's fears would not be put to rest. So, just to prove herself wrong, she decided to arrange a talk with her son.

One afternoon, after checking to see that he was there, she walked into his room with an armful of freshly pressed clothes. She hung his shirts and trousers in his closet, then handed him a stack of immaculately folded undergarments.

Jimmy laughed as he tucked them into a drawer. "Don't tell me you ironed these too," he said. Then, when she looked hurt, he added, "They look nice."

He returned to the mirror and began buttoning his shirt.

"You look pretty nice yourself," Haru said. "Where are you off to?"

He said, "I'm going over to Koba's—to hang out with him and his girlfriend—mmm, what's her name?"

"Missy," Haru said. "Missy, the Gravestone Carver's Daughter."

"Yeah, that's her," he said. "And then, the three of us will probably go for a bite somewhere. Maybe catch a movie."

She went to him and straightened his collar. "Why don't you wear one of the shirts I just ironed? This one's a little wrinkled," she said.

"It's okay," he answered. "We're not going any place dressy."

"Want me to give it a quick touch-up? It'll just take a minute."

"Relax, Ma. The shirt's fine," he said.

"Do you realize this is the longest conversation we've had since you've been back?" Haru said. She watched as he combed his hair. He'd always had such beautiful hair. "Do you have to go to Koba's today? Why don't you and I do something instead?"

"Like what?" he asked, inspecting his reflection.

Haru said, "Oh, go for a drive. I heard you tell Henry that you were finished working on the DeSoto. We can stop for dinner at one of the restaurants across the bay. Just the two of us. I'll take something out of the freezer for your father." She reached over and touched his arm. "How about it?"

He looked uneasy. "Right now, I've got this thing with Koba," he said.

"Is Lulu going to be there?" she asked.

"Oh, come on, Ma. Don't start on that," he said.

Haru persisted. "Well, is she?"

"How should I know?" he said, then took one of her hands. "We'll go for a drive tomorrow, okay?"

Haru saw him to the door. Then she pocketed her prayer beads and a newly cut *ti* leaf to ward off evil spirits, and set out after him down the road. It was half past six, and everyone was in their houses. She could hear oil frying and rice pots bubbling on kitchen stoves, and snippets of family conversations around dinner tables. She longed to be inside her own snug house, with a cup of tea and an after-dinner sweet instead of wandering a dusty road near nightfall when there were hungry ghosts about. All around her, their wispy forms loitered at windows and flitted beneath trees and hedges. She almost cried out when a large white dog crossed in front of her because she was sure it was the Guardian of the Dead warning her to go back.

Jimmy turned then, almost as if he'd heard the cry she hadn't made, and she slipped quickly behind a bush. She was sure he'd seen her, but he didn't stop. Her heart lifted when he marched past the corner where Lulu lived. By the time he turned in at Rusty Chan's Automotive Repair, Haru was wondering how she could ever have doubted him.

When she got there, the garage was locked and the office had a CLOSED sign in the window. She wandered out back, where she spotted Henry's DeSoto parked next to a banged-up station wagon at the far end of the lot. Jimmy had his back to her and was helping someone out of the car. Haru scooted forward for a better look, but she already knew who it was. She knew by the shaggy waist-length hair and tight black pedal pushers.

"So, is Koba going to cover for you if your mother gives him the third degree?" Lulu asked.

Jimmy's whole body had assumed a tense, listening pose, and he raised his hand to quiet her. "You hear anything out there?"

"It's probably rats," the girl said. "Come on, Jimmy, we don't have much time."

He listened for a second longer, then turned as she opened her arms to him. "Maybe we have more time than you think," he said.

She pulled away. "What do you mean? You told me you had to go back the end of this week."

"Maybe I'm not going back."

Haru inhaled sharply.

"Sure," the girl said. "Quit talking crazy."

"Well, maybe I'm not." Jimmy leaned back against the car and folded his arms. "Maybe I'm going to Canada."

Lulu looked up into his face and said, "Hey, you aren't kidding, are you?"

Jimmy said, "My pop went to pick up the ticket this afternoon. My reservation's for tomorrow at 3 P.M."

Haru closed her eyes. I am not hearing this, she thought. A terrible numbness began to spread through her chest.

"Tomorrow?" Lulu cried. "You can't go tomorrow. What about us?"

He tried to put his arms around her, but she pushed him away. "Come on, baby," he pleaded. "You know I'd never leave you behind." He murmured something else that Haru couldn't hear, and the girl murmured something back. The murmuring went on and on. There was the sound of a car door opening. "Oh, Lulu," he said. "Oh, Lulululu." He made her name sound like a song.

Haru got to her feet and began to stumble out the way she'd come. It was happening again, just like it had with Flora and Henry. Haru had been seeing him first, but it was Flora who'd gotten him—not so you'd notice she'd planned it, but by that slow, weaseling way she had. All her life she'd been a lingerer, dawdling over her food at meals, vacillating over what dress to buy in the Sears Roebuck catalogue, hanging on a man's every word. It had taken her six whole months to die. And now she continued lingering beyond the grave. Flora had weaseled her way into Henry's mind and was poisoning his thinking with her ghost schemes. It was Flora who had sent Lulu to lead Jimmy astray. Well, take the old man and good riddance, Haru thought, but the boy is mine. I haven't kept him safe all his life just to lose him like this.

Haru took the prayer beads from her pocket and began turning them in her hands. She had to think of something. Just up ahead, she could see the lights shining in the houses. As she drew closer to the Koyama Store, a purpose began to form in her mind. Downstairs, the windows were dark, but she could see Lulu's grandmother moving around inside. She went to the door and began to knock.

Henry counted out the fifties and hundreds into crisp stacks on his desk and laid the airplane ticket next to them. All in a good day's work, he thought. Down the hall, he could hear the back door open, then close. He paused, listening. "Jimmy," he called. "Is that you?" He slipped the money and the ticket into a drawer, then went out into the living room.

Haru was sitting on the couch in the dark. "How long have you been home?" she asked.

"The bus just dropped me off," he said, settling into an armchair across from her. He reached up to switch on the floor lamp.

"I've come from the repair shop," she said. "Jimmy's finished the car."

He said, "I know; I was the one who told you that. What were you doing wandering around this time of night by yourself?" A suspicious look crossed his face. "Have you been spying again?"

"Maybe I was." She looked down at her hands, then up at him again.

"Christ, Haru," he began.

"I know about Canada," she said.

He tried to swallow, but his mouth had suddenly turned dry. When he spoke again, his voice was hoarse. "What do you mean, you *know?*"

"I mean I know everything," she said. "And so does Lulu's grandmother and sister, and Emi McAllister, and the head priest's wife, and everyone who was at tonight's meeting of the Ladies Auxiliary. I'd think twice about giving Jimmy that airplane ticket you went into town to pick up today."

Henry covered his face with his hands. He was back in the hills of Okinawa. He was standing at the opening to a cave and piling it with rocks. The rocks were heavy, and their jagged surfaces bit into his palms. He could hear his gunnery sergeant yelling, "Hurry up and get out of there, you crazy Jap!" But he didn't hurry; he wanted time, and there was no time. He looked at Haru. "Why?" he asked. "What have you gone and done?"

"I've put everything back where it belongs," she said, then brushed past him and stepped outside. There was the smell of ocean in the air. Down the road, voices called, screen doors slammed, pots and pans clattered, incense burned, and the ghosts ate quietly, quietly as the darkness closed over her, familiar and safe.

Certainty

Though he had his back to Lily, the man at the phone booth seemed about her father's age, with the same brownish hair and angular build. As she gazed at him across the bright pavement, she began to feel dizzy with the light. Then he turned and headed toward the picnic table where she and her mother were lunching. When he drew closer and Lily was able to make out his face, the likeness dissolved. She shut her eyes and waited for the dizziness to pass. Behind her closed lids, she could see the gold trees above her burning like candles against the sky.

Her mother said, "Are you all right? I might have told you it wasn't him."

The candles went out.

"I don't know what I was thinking," Lily said, though this had not been the first time she'd imagined seeing him. Just the week before, she'd thought she'd spotted him unloading a boat down at the harbor.

From her wheelchair at the head of the table, her mother began clearing away the debris from lunch. She gathered the trash into a pile and folded all the aluminum foil and plastic wrap. She replaced the lids on the jars of condiments and containers of fried chicken and potato salad, then started packing the leftovers into the basket. She worked in silence, occasionally taking things out and repositioning them. Suddenly, after struggling with a jar of sweet pickles that wouldn't fit, she flung it to the ground and cried, "It's been almost fifteen years, how long does it take to be free of that man?"

The clouds overhead were gathering fast when they pulled in at the Laniloa Geriatric Care Facility. Lily's mother had not spoken since her outburst at the park, and she maintained her silence while Lily helped her out of the back seat and into her wheelchair.

They made it to the lobby just as the first drops began to fall. At the reception desk Lily hesitated, wondering if she should ask whether a single room had come available, but decided against it after glimpsing her mother's stony expression. Lily's queasiness had begun to return. Familiarity with her mother's silences had not made them less unsettling.

They passed through a corridor lined with old women.

Some sat with their heads down, staring, neither awake nor asleep. Others were twisted with bone disease—their hands like tightly curled buds waiting to bloom. Here and there, a limb twitched uncontrollably or a mouth worked without emitting any sound.

"Despite early periods of remission, the disease is progressive," Lily remembered the doctor saying.

"Driftwood," her mother whispered.

When they arrived at her room, she wheeled over to the inert form in the bed next to hers and exclaimed, "Look at that. Eyes turned clean up to the top of her head. Except for the snoring, you can't tell she's alive." Then she turned to Lily and asked, "Back at the reception desk, why didn't you find out when I could move?"

It was still drizzling when Lily returned to her car. The weather and the view of the harbor from the parking lot again reminded her of her father. As she drove past the boats at their moorings, she remembered how he'd batten down the *Mele* on stormy days, then cancel his sightseeing cruises while they went on Jack Daniels walks to hunt driftwood in the rain.

After they'd gone a distance, he'd pick out a twisted branch, bleached white and smooth as bone, and stand over it, taking long pulls from his flask. "What do you think?" he'd finally say, then kneel beside her while she considered the figures in the grain—the mermaids, angels, and dancing ladies—that had been put there by the sea and by time. "Looks like one for the Treasure House," she'd agree, and they'd lift the branch to their shoulders and haul it home.

The Treasure House was a storage shed in their backyard, which Pop always kept locked and for which he had the only key. The "bone pile," Mama called it. When he'd disappear out there for hours, working on the carvings he kept a secret from everyone, she'd say, "Mr. Sawbones is sitting on his bone pile." The more time he spent in the Treasure House, the sharper Mama's tongue became, until both he and Lily grew wary of getting caught on the wrong side of it.

Sometimes after a day of sightseeing cruises, Pop didn't come home, and those nights Mama would go about her chores fuming silently until, suddenly, she'd smash the crockery drying on the sink or hurl the flowers she'd been arranging across the room. After a while, she stopped speaking to Pop at all—except indirectly through Lily. "Ask Mr. Sawbones if he might interrupt his chewing to pass the salt," she'd say. Or "Please inform Mr. Sawbones that the gasoline bill for his pleasure cruiser has not been paid for the month of June." One day, Lily went down to his boat and discovered that he'd painted *Aloha* in front of *Mele,* her mother's name.

Though she wasn't certain what happened next, she recalled accompanying him down to the pier the following morning. As they walked out over the water, the sun was coming up and the air was turning to rose. She stood watching as he unlashed the boat and pulled up anchor. When he finished, he said, "If that old woman had her way, she'd put out the stars." Then, he guided the *Aloha Mele* out of the harbor, and sailed farther and farther, until he was only a yellow speck of light upon the sea.

When Lily arrived at her husband's hardware store, the closed sign was in the window, but she could see him working at his desk in back. She tapped at the glass to catch his attention, then waited out of the rain while he came to let her in.

"I'll be done in a minute," he said, heading back to his books.

"Busy day?" she called after him, but he was already bent over his adding machine.

While she was waiting, she wandered the aisles—past shelves of house paint and motorized lawn equipment, racks of screwdrivers and wrenches, bins filled with different sizes and types of small metal objects. Things were meticulously arranged by function and labeled, which did not make them any less incomprehensible. Hardware would be mysterious if it weren't so boring, she thought.

She glanced down a row of electrical wiring supplies at the balding, slightly paunchy figure of her husband adding up the day's receipts. She remembered how they met her first summer home from college when she'd worked at the bakery a few doors away. He came in once a day at first, then twice, and she'd thought him uncommonly fond of chocolate doughnuts. But after a while, he began asking her to the movies and out for drives, which she'd found pleasant, though he'd never had much to say. As the end of her vacation neared and she tried to think of a way to tell her mother that she didn't want to return to school, Clyde had asked her to marry him. To her surprise, her mother had encouraged the match. "If you don't intend to finish college," she'd said, with her usual ability to read Lily's mind, "you could probably benefit from his sense of organization." Having no other plans, Lily had said yes to him.

While Lily prepared dinner, Clyde sat in his underwear at the kitchen table and read the news.

"I saw my mother today," she said, putting the chicken pies in the oven. When he didn't answer, she repeated herself. "Did you hear me? I saw my mother."

"And how's she doing? She asking to come home?" he asked, still reading.

"No, Mother would never ask that," she answered.

"I guess she wouldn't," he said.

She began shredding lettuce for the salad. "Still, I hate to see her in that place. She's plenty sharp, and she seems to be feeling stronger again."

He looked up then, and said, "You thinking of bringing her back?"

She said, "I know Mother can be difficult."

"That's not the point," he said. "Remember the last time she got so sick?"

Lily remembered. How sensible he was. Then, ashamed of her relief, she murmured, "I've been feeling a bit under the weather myself," but he had already returned to his paper.

Lily finished toweling herself dry, then slipped into her thick, terry cloth robe. Before reaching for the jar of night cream on the bathroom vanity, she paused to wipe away the condensation on the mirror, and stood for a second, contemplating her reflection. The high forehead. The fair skin. The light brown hair tinged with red. Her father's *haole* forehead and skin and hair. "Windowdressing," her mother called it. "Inside, your bones are Hawaiian. And your mouth and nose are from your great grandmother Kanahele, who could talk her way out of anything and sniff trouble a mile away. A nose like that is a real gift. I didn't have it, and that's how I ended up as I did."

Lily switched off the bathroom light and padded into the bedroom. After hanging up her robe, she went to the dresser and pulled on an undershirt, a pair of flannel pajama bottoms, and a long flannel nightgown.

"How can you sleep with all that paraphernalia?" Clyde asked as she perched on the edge of the bed, putting on a pair of socks. "It must be eighty degrees in here."

The rain had finally stopped, and the smell of plumeria seeped through the cracks in the walls, the floorboards, and ceiling. "Lately, I get chilled from the damp," she answered. "Besides, you're the one who always complains about my cold feet."

Clyde pulled her down next to him.

"Hmm, cold feet," he said when she stopped him from unbuttoning her nightgown. Her breasts hurt, and she did not like to have them touched.

"I feel sick," she said, then got out of bed and went back into the bathroom.

"Did I ask for this?" She could hear him muttering down the hall to the kitchen. There was the squeak of the refrigerator door and the hiss of a bottle cap being opened. Then, silence. Lily sat on the bathroom floor with her head on her knees.

"Hey, Lil, you okay in there?" Clyde tapped on the door.

"Go away," she said.

And he did.

"Clyde?" She turned to him in her sleep.

The phone was ringing, and the sheets on his side of the bed were already cold. When she reached for the receiver, the line went dead.

Lily got to her feet and shuffled groggily down the hall. Her head ached and her stomach still felt a little upset. The kitchen was filled with the smell of fried bacon. After opening the windows and putting the kettle on for tea, she discovered Clyde's note on the message board attached to the refrigerator. "Better see doctor," it said.

Better than what? Lily thought. For the past few weeks, she had excised the word "baby" from her vocabulary. She sat for a while sipping her tea, then reached for the phone and began dialing Doc McAllister's number. Her hands were trembling. As soon as the phone began ringing, she hung up.

"*Lilia*—a lily. *Lele*—to fly." She remembered her father's teasing voice. "Where flies my Lily in the sky?" She remembered a clear morning down at the harbor, the air the color of rose.

The phone was ringing again when she got out of the shower, and for a second she hesitated, thinking Doc McAllister had somehow traced her call. But it was Hattie McPherson, the social worker at the Laniloa.

They met in front of the reception desk. "We've been having a minor, well, a problem with—logistics," Miss McPherson began. She was a small, tremulous person with a disconcerting way of fixing you with her left eye while her right gazed dreamily at a corner of the ceiling. "A private room became available, and we were moving your mother, just as she'd requested—"

"You might have called me first," Lily murmured.

"Well, I did, several times, before I finally reached you. It's a miracle she was able to get a single at all. And such a nice room too, up on the eighth floor. It even has a view."

"You mentioned some problem?" Lily interjected.

"Yes, so I did. I didn't actually see what happened, but the nurse on duty told the head RN that they had taken your mother up to the new room and had lifted her onto the bed when she began causing a fuss and, well, I hate to say, but it finally took two nurses and the cleaning woman to hold her down."

Lily said, "They did what?"

"As I've told you, I wasn't there," Miss McPherson said. "But the staff on the scene had to restrain her."

"Where is my mother now?" Lily asked.

"She's still up there. But we—the administration and I —thought you might talk to her and find out how genuine, that is, how interested she is in moving to a single. Otherwise, you realize, we have other clients who would appreciate knowing one is available."

Lily found her mother outside the door to her new room. She was dozing, with her wrists strapped to the arms of her wheelchair. As Lily knelt beside her to undo the restraints, her mother opened her eyes. "What are you doing here?" she asked.

Lily got to her feet and said, "The social worker called me. She said there was some sort of misunderstanding about your moving rooms—"

"I want to go home," her mother interrupted. When Lily didn't answer, she said, "Then, I want to go back to my old room. This one won't do." She seemed distracted. "Go on inside and see for yourself."

From the paint on the walls to the arrangement of the furniture, the new room seemed, at first glance, identical to the old. Lily said, "It's the same, Mama."

"Look harder," her mother said. "The window. Don't you *see?*"

Still puzzled, Lily turned and finally saw—the harbor below, and beyond it, the ocean.

Her mother said, "Every time I looked out that window, I'd remember *him.*"

"I remember," Lily whispered. "I remember all the time."

"And just what is that?" her mother cried. "Some fairytale about how he climbed into his boat one morning and went sailing off into the sunrise?" She had wheeled into the room and was right behind Lily. "Come on, girl, think back."

Lily felt one of her bad spells coming on. "If you don't like it here," she said, "there's no reason you have to stay. I'll see the social worker right now." She turned to leave, but her mother was in the way.

"Think back, Lily," she repeated. "It was still dark. Around three in the morning. Don't you remember? You'd wakened with a bad dream, and I'd just gotten you to go back to bed when we heard him come in."

"I'm not listening to this." Lily tried to push past, but her mother wouldn't let her.

"Remember?" she insisted. "The wind was blowing something fierce." Her words conjured the memory of the red dirt swirling in the yellow light of the porch.

Lily closed her eyes. She remembered the banging of the wind against the shutters and the sound of singing out in the yard.

"I always knew when he was near," her mother continued. "No matter how quiet he was, I could tell when he came sneaking back to the shed. Night after night, while he was out there, I'd lie awake waiting. That morning, for the first time, he didn't bother hiding what he was up to, and I'd had enough."

Lily remembered following her mother into the garage, then watching as she unhooked the crowbar from the wall. "No," Lily had screamed, trying to pull her back. Now she covered her ears with her hands. "It was a clear summer morning," she chanted. "Early, when the sun was rising above the hills."

But her mother pulled her arms down and continued gripping her by the wrists. "We went around to the backyard," she said, "and you struggled to stop me.

"But I circled that shed and smashed its black-tarred windows, one by one. Then I used every bit of strength I had left and pried open the door."

As her mother spoke, Lily was standing once again in front of the shed. She could hear the groan of metal, as the door to the Treasure House began to give. She wanted to look away, but she could not. Slowly, the opening widened, until finally she could see inside. She could see the stacks of driftwood, just as they'd been dragged in from the sea. No mermaids or dancing ladies, only bleached white bone. And there, in the middle of the floor . . .

Her mother said, "I can still see them, stupid with drink—your father and his fat pink whore."

She was staring past Lily at the harbor. Her hair, lit by the sun, was silver against her dark skin. Her face was drawn. "They headed for the boat," she went on, "and you followed them. I caught you halfway up the pier just as they were pulling away." Exhausted, she let go of Lily's wrists, and they remained for a while without talking.

Then Lily said, "Did you ever hear from him?"

"What do you think?" her mother said.

"I always thought he'd come back," Lily answered.

Her mother sighed. It cost her an effort to speak. "I know that," she said. "But now with the baby coming,

maybe you'll have enough to keep you busy, and I can
finally get some peace."

Lily didn't know how long she'd been sitting, but it was
already afternoon. She remembered that she still had to
shop for dinner, then got to her feet and started back across
the park. She passed a group of children playing a make-
shift game of football, a couple of suntanners, the phone
booth where she'd imagined seeing her father. He was still
somewhere out there, the thought rose unbidden. And for a
second she felt, or perhaps just imagined, a tentative fluttering in her belly. Suddenly, there was a flash of silver
overhead, and a flock of pigeons circled past. "Here chick!
Here chick!" someone behind her called. She turned and
saw an old man in yellow golf pants, throwing bread at the
sky.

A Summer Waltz

The last day of summer. Even before Sachi opened her
eyes, she knew it was fine—blindly, through her skin, from
the warmth in the air and the sound of the birds. The
doves always launched into a frenzy of cooing on overcast
mornings before the rain; today they were still. Outside, the
sky was blue, and all the hours in the day belonged to her.

Sachi pulled on a pair of jeans and a shirt, grabbed a
sweet bun from the tray on the kitchen counter, and raced
past her mother hanging the wash in the backyard. "Mind
yourself!" her mother called. She gestured in the direction
of the rabbit hutches next to the garage. "You be sure to get
home in time to feed those beasts." But the words evapo-

rated in the bright air, as Sachi jumped on her bike and headed for Meg Finnegan's.

She pedaled down the red dirt road—past the grave-yard, the Koyama Store, and the turnoff for Dead Man's Slide. She pedaled away from the sugar mill, the identical green and white company houses, and the Japanese school to which, even in summer, she had to go each Wednesday and Friday afternoon. Outside the village, she turned off the dirt road onto the blacktop and began climbing the big hill where the Bird Lady lived in her stone house overlook-ing the sea. Meg lived on the other side, at the bottom of the winding road that led to the country club.

Shortly after Meg's parents took out a membership in early June, the girls had celebrated their seventh birthdays, which were three days apart, at the clubhouse restaurant. During the remainder of the vacation, now drawing to an end, Mr. Finnegan had been teaching them to swim at the pool. Once a week, Sachi had followed her friend into the water—the way they took turns following one another on various occasions—with a kind of blind faith, as Meg splashed wildly toward the sound of her father's voice yell-ing encouragement from the deep end.

From the very first, Mr. and Mrs. Finnegan had forbid-den them to visit the club without a grown-up chaperone. This restriction merely added to the club's allure—a pull which Meg and Sachi felt most strongly on nights when the air was fragrant with plumeria and the first strains from the dance band drifted down the hill toward the Finnegans' house. Then the girls would go out onto the patio and watch the torches around the dance floor light up, one by one. In the distance, they looked like birthday candles burning all night long.

At first Sachi and Meg had been content to dress up in

Mrs. Finnegan's old evening gowns and parade across the lawn with their oversized skirts trailing on the grass. Meg, whose favorite color was pink, always chose the rose-colored taffeta with a wide skirt and puffy sleeves, while Sachi, who liked green best, never wore anything but the emerald satin with a sequined top. "We're off to the club now!" they'd call to Meg's mother, just as she had called to them a hundred times, and she'd look up from mixing the pie dough or weeding the honeysuckle and say to be back in time for supper and not to slam the door when they got in.

All vacation long, the girls had been content to act out their make-believe in the carport, which stood empty while Mr. Finnegan was away at work. But on the last day of summer, when they called out that they were "off to the club," one of them—Meg swore it was Sachi, and Sachi, Meg—began to head up the hill, with the other following as usual, not far behind. Decked out in Mrs. Finnegan's castoff finery and high-heeled shoes, with their nickels for the ice cream man jingling in their pockets, they felt suddenly free.

"What can I do for you ladies?" asked the thin, middle-aged man behind the clubhouse bar. It was midmorning and the place was empty. The man had a kindly face and sandy hair. When the girls walked in, he had been looking over the bottles behind the counter and writing some figures in a book. Meg and Sachi nudged one another, then said, "Two strawberry sodas, please."

The man's gaze suddenly sharpened, and for a guilt-stricken moment Sachi imagined that he was going to remind them not to eat any sweets before lunch. Instead, he said, "Strawberry sodas? After you've been out dancing all night? I think that you each need a stiff tomato juice cocktail, at the very least."

This was not how it was supposed to go. Sachi felt sick. Meg was beginning to look panicky.

"Or perhaps a Shirley Temple," the man suggested.

Sachi was still suspicious. "Does it have any vegetables in it?"

"Absolutely," the man said gravely. "It's made out of onionskins and artichoke fur—artichokes grow fur all over their tongues because they drink too much, did you know that?—but it's terrific for a hangover. Now, go and sit over there while I mix your cocktails." He gestured them toward one of the tables.

"I'm getting out of here," Meg said in a tentative way, and Sachi nodded. Neither of them budged.

In a few minutes, the man came over to their table carrying two wonderfully garish, pink-colored drinks. Each glass was festooned with a maraschino cherry, a miniature paper umbrella, and a menagerie of tiny plastic animals clinging by various appendages to the rim.

"It's obviously someone's birthday," the man said.

Neither of them corrected him. Instead, Meg pointed at Sachi. "Hers," she fibbed.

"It's not," Sachi denied. Then she smiled and declared triumphantly, "It's both!"

"Ah, twins," the man said, delighting them all over again. Then he extended one hand toward Sachi and the other toward Meg. "May I have this dance?" he asked.

"But there's no music," Meg, who should have known better, protested.

The man replied, "There's always music." And as he hummed the opening bars of "Alice Blue Gown," the three joined hands and waltzed around, and around, and around the empty floor.

A Spell of Kona Weather

For a couple of months after my sister Lulu ran Henry Hanabusa's '49 DeSoto into the tree at the bottom of Dead Man's Slide, she had to go to Doc McAllister's once a week to get the glass picked out of her face. Every Saturday morning, after she came home from the hospital, I walked her to his surgery in the big white house across the road, and then stood with my eyes shut, squeezing her hand, as he picked the slivers out with a pair of pointed stainless steel tweezers.

The accident had happened in April, the night she found out that Henry's son Jimmy had been killed in Vietnam. Jimmy and she had been going together since their senior year in high school, and his mother had always had about as much use for Lulu as our grandmother had for him. At any rate, Lulu didn't get the news of his death till nearly a week later when she overheard a couple of customers gossiping during her shift at Grandmother's store. That night, after she'd finished work, she stole over to the Hanabusa house and hot-wired Jimmy's father's DeSoto. She told me later that she and Jimmy had spent almost every minute of his last R and R working on that damn thing, and according to her calculations of time put in, it was more hers than anyone else's. After she got it started, she drove to the top of Dead Man's Slide, turned off the ignition, and let out the brake. For a couple of seconds, she said, she had the highest high she'd ever had.

On the day when Lulu's bandages came off, Grandmother locked up the grocery and accompanied us to Doc's for the first and last time. Dressed all in black, with her black-dyed hair pulled tightly into a bun, she looked like she was going to someone's funeral. When my sister emerged from the examining room, the old lady took in the damage with that measuring gaze of hers. Lulu had never been a beauty, but she had had a kind of vividness that almost made you think she was—with her brown skin, and black hair, and large dark eyes. Now, much of her face was still badly bruised. There were small gashes all over her cheeks and lips, and a row of stitches extended along one side of her jaw to her chin.

"Lucky nothing was broken. Just give it time," Doc said, putting the bandages aside and gently smoothing Lulu's rumpled hair, still as long and glossy as ever—so strangely untouched.

Grandmother got to her feet, then said, "There's nothing to be done. It's too broken to fix."

With that assessment, she abandoned years of trying to put my sister right. Once, when I asked the old lady exactly what she thought was wrong with Lulu, she'd said, "If you were a perfect stranger, would you ever guess that that girl was a granddaughter of mine?" I have always considered it my bad luck that no one could mistake me for anything else. Lulu gets her looks from our father, on the Amalu side of the family. I take after the tight-lipped, narrow-eyed Koyamas. When we were going to school, Lulu was called fast, and it wasn't for her brain. I was a plodder who got good grades. She is "wild" like our mama was. My middle name is Caution.

The one advantage I ever got from all this was that Grandmother left me alone the whole time she was sending my sister off to learn kimono wearing, or tea pouring, or pigeon-toed walking at the deportment classes sponsored by the Buddhist Mission's Ladies Auxiliary. If this reform program worked, Grandmother had believed, she could eventually hook Lulu up with some Nice Young Man, like Clyde Sakamoto, who had recently inherited his father's hardware business, or Mrs. Kobayashi's cousin's friend's son who was opening a dermatology practice in the resort town nearby. According to Grandmother's standards, Jimmy did not qualify as a Nice Young Man. He belonged to another category called Bad Influences. I never had anything against him, though. It seemed Lulu had found something in him that she'd always been looking for.

Before Lulu met Jimmy, she used to drive me crazy with her talk about finding our mama. Sometimes, when she got fed up with Grandmother's meddling, she'd do more than talk, she'd run away, then Grandmother would call in the authorities to haul her back. Once, to teach Lulu a lesson, the old lady even had her put in the Girls' Detention Home over at the county seat. For a while, all that stopped when my sister was with Jimmy.

Personally, I can't say I ever understood Lulu's obsession with Mama, especially since I can't remember a thing. Papa died when I was just a few years old, and our mother took off for California not long after. As the old saying goes, out of sight, out of mind; that's pretty much how it's been with me.

Lulu is only two years older than I am and can't claim much more of a memory. Still, while we were growing up, she tried to convince me that grief had driven Mama away, and that she'd send for us once she was feeling herself again. But when our mother went off, she left everything, except the five thousand dollars from our father's insurance policy, behind with our grandmother—a sure sign, I'd decided when I was old enough to figure things out, that she'd never intended to return. Besides, if someone ups and leaves for sixteen years and you don't hear anything from them except an occasional store-bought greeting with no return address, you figure they're trying to tell you something, and it isn't Dying to See You, Please Come Soon. For the last five years or so, we haven't heard a single word.

With Jimmy's death and then the accident, I was afraid that the old craziness would start up again. But Lulu seemed to have left all that behind. After her visits to Doc's had ended, and her face had started returning to normal, she began going for long swims out in the bay. Though she hadn't gotten her old looks back, she wasn't exactly at a loss. Several times, I saw her with a white guy. I saw him running after her on the sand, catching her, brushing back her hair with his hands. You could tell by the way he moved that he was older than the surfers who usually hang out at the beach, and there was something familiar about him, though I'd never gotten close enough to find out what.

Then, a couple of weeks ago, Lulu asked me to go with her. There's almost nothing I hate worse than ocean swimming—with the sting of salt in your eyes and the live feel of the water. But I know that Lulu knows that about me, so I make it a point never to refuse her invitations. That day, I followed her into the surf where it broke high up on the beach and swirled around our legs, pulling us deeper and deeper until the ocean bottom suddenly dropped off into nothing. Beneath the surface, I felt the current pulling at me, and fear tightened my chest. We swam out to the raft about a hundred yards from shore and stayed there talking awhile before turning back.

She told me about the man I'd seen her with. "It isn't like it was with Jimmy," she said. "But after his divorce, we'll move to the West Coast, and maybe I can even get one of those plastic surgeons there to fix my face."

I said, "You mean he's *married*? How do you know he's going to leave his wife?"

"I just know," she answered, and smiled dreamily.

"But did he actually come out and say so?" I demanded.

She snapped, "Not in so many words. You've got to read between the lines." She sat up and put her legs in the water. "Annie, do you know what your problem is? You've got no imagination."

"And maybe you have too much of one," I said. But she was already swimming back toward shore.

After that day, she didn't bring up the subject again, though I continued to go with her on her swims. Each time we swam farther and farther, until one afternoon we reached the buoy at the center of the bay. The currents were stronger there, and ran deeper, and if you fitted yourself into the wrong channel by mistake, or if you went out between tides, you could be swept into the open sea. As I stroked out toward the buoy, I fought down the voice in my head screaming to turn back.

Then, a couple of days ago, she did not turn around. I stopped and clung to the buoy as it bobbed up and down, and I watched her moving, strong and smooth, away from me. When I could hardly see her anymore, I turned and headed for the beach, now more afraid of the ocean than of Lulu.

She took a long time swimming back, and stumbled out of the surf, nearly falling. When she saw me watching her, she broke into a run. She gasped, "Annie, you chicken. I turned to look for you, and you weren't there."

As she sat catching her breath, I asked, "You been seeing that guy?"

Lulu laughed. "Sure have. He's crazy about me." She looked out over the water. "But not crazy enough to ditch his wife."

Around us, in the gathering dark, the afternoon had turned to lead. The sky and the sea had become the same dull shade of gray, and you couldn't tell where one began and the other ended.

"So, aren't you going to say, 'I told you so'?" she finally said. I looked down and began digging at the sand with a stick. She tossed back her hair. "Who needs him anyway?" She gave me a sly, triumphant look. "This morning I got a

letter from Mama. She's moved to Oregon, and she wants
me to join her."

I began to protest, but I looked at her face just then and
stopped. Instead, I said, "What are you going to do for a
plane ticket?"

She gave me a pitying look. "Poor Annie," she said.
"Always the businesswoman."

Yesterday morning, when Lulu was supposed to be working at the store, she emptied the cash register. Grandmother put Sheriff Kanoi on her, and he found her a few
hours later, full of vodka and 7-Up, at the La Hula
Rhumba Bar and Grill. After he'd brought her back and
I'd put her to bed upstairs, the old lady and I sat outside on
the front steps with sodas.

Grandmother swallowed the last of her root beer and
set down the bottle. "If that girl doesn't get hold of herself,
she's going to end up in a crazy house, just like your
mama."

When she said that, she caught me off balance the way
she and Lulu are always so good at; and, for a second, I
couldn't believe I'd heard what I did. "What're you talking
about?" I finally said. "Mama's in Oregon."

She stood and started up the steps. "That's just another
of your sister's stories."

I knew it was, but I wasn't admitting anything. "What
about California?" I cried. "She sent us birthday cards.
That wasn't a story."

Grandmother turned back toward me, then said, "No,
she was in California all right. Still is. But what do you
suppose she's been doing there? She went nuts after your

father died; that man had such a hold on her, I never
understood it." She sighed. "From what I've heard, they
shot her brain full of electricity a few years back, and she
hasn't done much letter writing since."

I was so stunned, at first, I couldn't move. Then I
threw my soda at her. She ducked as it went past, and the
bottle crashed against the wall and broke, spewing root
beer across the porch.

Grandmother stepped around the puddles of soda and
broken glass. "You be sure and clean up that mess," she
called over her shoulder as she pushed open the door to the
grocery and went inside.

Upstairs, the screen door slammed, and there was the
sound of footsteps on the stairs. I knew that Lulu must
have heard.

"Lulu!" I called as she headed down the road to the
beach. "Where're you headed?" She began walking even
faster in the direction of the water. I could see the old lady
at the back of the store, closing up the register, but I didn't
say anything, and took off after my sister.

When I got to the beach, it was deserted, and the tide
was going out. "Lulu!" I shouted again, but she ignored
me. I was still feeling tired from the previous day's swim,
and shouting only used up breath.

The sand pulled at my legs. My chest burned. I stumbled and nearly fell, but I was gaining on her. She was so
close—just ahead, at the edge of the water. Oh, please, I
thought, please let me reach her before we have to start
swimming. The waves fanned out across the sand, pulling
at my ankles. Lulu was about ten feet away. Then, suddenly, she seemed to drop off the edge of the world. I saw
her head bobbing above the water, and I knew I had to go
in too. I waded in, feeling sand under my feet, and sand,

and sand, then nothing. The ocean was unbearably alive around me, the pull of the current strong. I swam toward Lulu, closed on her, reached, and missed. The movement disrupted the rhythm of our strokes. We flailed around for a little, trying to pick it up again.

"Go back," she gasped. I reached for her, and she repeated, "Go back."

I reached a third time and got her. She struggled. We both went under. She stopped fighting. We were almost at the raft; then we were there. We pulled ourselves onto it and lay, panting, with our heads on our arms. For a long time we were too spent to talk. When we'd recovered a little, she said she'd return with me; maybe she knew I wouldn't make it if I had to pull her in.

We swam across the current to get back to shore and crawled out onto the beach. As we rested, side by side, I kept remembering how it was when we were kids—the way she'd marched straight into things, while I tagged along. "Are you sure, Lulu? Is it safe?" But I'd followed, afraid of what lay ahead—the top branch of the mango tree in the graveyard, Dead Man's Slide in the dark, the deep water out beyond the buoy—but more afraid to be left behind.

I reached over and touched her face with my fingers. I could still feel the hard lumps under her skin where the fragments of glass sometimes came poking through. She opened her eyes and smiled. "I bet I could have made it clear to the other side," she said.

During the night the wind shifted to the southeast, and the Kona weather moved in. Now the wet, still air presses close, heavy with the threat of rain. My sister has stayed

upstairs and slept all day. Whenever I look at my grandmother's face or hear her voice, I think of the pistols I saw
once in a glass cabinet at the Sakamoto Hardware, and I
imagine picking one of them up in my hand, and feeling
the weight of it, and slowly easing the trigger back.

"It's better if Lulu goes away for a little while," Grandmother says from across the store. Her angular shape pokes
out from behind the cash register—her black dress, blacker
than the shadows around her. "Doc McAllister's told me he
knows a place where they will give her proper care."

You mean, like they did to Mama? I want to say. Instead, I pick up a rag and begin dusting the jars of colored
puffed rice, preserved plums, and dried cuttlefish lined up
on tiers across from where she's sitting. Beads of moisture
drop from my forehead onto the heavy glass lids.

Grandmother finishes counting out the cash in the register, and slips it into a bank bag. "There's nothing more to
be done," she says.

Upstairs, Lulu has wakened and is moving around. It is
the sound I have been listening for. "You finished counting
the money?" I ask, a little too loudly. The screen door
bangs softly, as if a breeze is pushing at it, but there is no
breeze. There is the sound of footsteps on the stairs.

Grandmother is halfway to the door, then turns. "You
saw me," she says. "Do you need glasses?" The footsteps
move across the drive and out into the road.

I say, "You're right. I forgot. Shall I close up now?"

"There's no need to shout." The old lady waves impa-
tiently, muttering, "Do what you like," and lets herself out.

When she is gone, I switch off the lights and sit for a
while, listening.

The Ghost of Fred Astaire

After Great Uncle Kazuhiro Sato died, his daughter Minerva returned to the village to claim her inheritance—a run-down two-story rooming house called the Bachelor Palms. Grandmother says that the place started going to seed when the Paradise Mortuary opened next door and it became rumored that the spirits of the newly departed were taking up residence in Great Uncle's establishment. Up until then, he and his wife, Grandmother's younger sister Miho, had run a prosperous business providing for the single, mostly Filipino men who worked on the nearby sugar plantation. For thirty-five years, until she expired in the midst of preparing a Thanksgiving dinner, Aunt Miho cooked over a hundred meals a day. "Someday all this will be yours," Great Uncle promised Cousin Minerva. But the summer she turned eighteen, Minerva ran away from all that cooking to pursue a tap dancing career in Hollywood.

"It was like stabbing the old man through the heart," Grandmother says with her usual knack for understatement. And that wasn't the worst of it. The whole time Great Uncle was threatening to disown their daughter, Aunt Miho was supplying her with funds enclosed in notes that said, "Be a success. If you come back, I'll never forgive you." When Minerva finally realized that Hollywood didn't offer much of a market for female Japanese American impersonators of Fred Astaire, Aunt Miho wrote her, "Don't give up. This is a free country. You can be anything you want."

Cousin Minerva was inspired by her mother's advice. She moved to San Francisco and changed her name to Mi Ho Min. She learned Chinese. She auditioned for Sinbad Ah Soon's All-Girl Revue at the Seven Happiness Nightclub in Chinatown. After she was hired on, she sent home photos of herself with the other girls in the show. "Here I am with Ginger Rogers Wong," the captions on back of the pictures said. "This is me with the Mae West of the East." She mailed her mother an airplane ticket to come see her perform, but Great Uncle wouldn't hear of it. Then, a few years later when Aunt Miho died, Min did not return for the funeral. For a long time, the rest of the family lost track of her—though for a while following Pearl Harbor, a rumor circulated through the village that she had escaped being interned and was enjoying a prosperous nightclub career under her newly acquired identity.

"It was just a rumor," Mother reminds us whenever Grandmother tells this story.

But Grandmother says that no form of underhandedness is beyond someone without a sense of Filial Obligation.

"Aunt Miho didn't see it that way," Mother objects.

"Your Aunt Miho was a foolish woman," Grandmother replies.

Personally, I don't much care about the family politics. I am more interested in getting the facts straight. For instance, where did Cousin Min learn to tap dance? And just how good was her Chinese?

Whenever I bring up these questions, Mother says, "The only fact you need to remember is that Minerva is a member of this family."

After Great Uncle died without a will, it was Mother who hired the detective agency which traced Cousin Min to the retirement home in Santa Monica. She spoke to Min on the phone a couple of times but couldn't persuade her to return, and Grandmother began talking about selling the Palms to one of the Canadian or Japanese real estate companies which were scouting out property around the village. "Let *them* worry about the ghosts," she said. Then, one evening, as we were sitting down to dinner, an airport taxi stopped in front of the house.

Our father pushed through the screen door and stepped out onto the porch—the rest of us not far behind. "You looking for someone?" he asked.

The cab door opened, and a slim figure in a white linen suit and straw Panama got out.

"Wow," my sister Ruby whispered.

"Don't stare," I whispered back, staring. I felt uneasy, as if I were looking at something I couldn't name.

"Well," Grandmother said. "Minerva Sato."

I noticed that Pearlie Woo had also come out across the road and was gesturing at her husband inside their house. Pearlie's neighbor Haru Hanabusa looked up from watering her ginger bushes and did not look away. From all over the neighborhood, I could feel people's eyes on us.

"Cousin Min, so good to see you," Mother called. She pushed our father forward. "Need help with your luggage?"

Min said, "I wouldn't mind a hand, though that one case is all I brought." Father went around to the back of the cab where the driver was struggling to unload an enormous steamer trunk. Between the two of them, they managed to get it out of the car and grunt it up the walk onto the porch. "I can take it from here," Father said, staggering into the house.

Cousin Min paid the driver. Then she turned toward us and took off her hat. Her hair was white and cut as short as a man's. Her skin was the color of parchment. She went to Mother and they put their arms around each other like old friends—the one so tall and pale, the other short and dark. For an instant, I didn't know why, I wanted to run down there and pull them apart.

If I believed in intuition, I might say I had it then, though Ruby blames my aversion to Cousin Min on a disinclination to anything new. Of course, that's not the way she puts it; she calls me a stick-in-the-mud. Maybe that's true, if it means that I want things to be orderly, that I like them to add up. But as I've said before, there are too many things about Cousin Min that do not.

Then, there were the small inconveniences. Father

threw his back out trying to haul her trunk up the stairs and ended up missing work for nearly a week, which he spent yelling orders at me from the living room couch. Mother began serving breakfast for dinner because Cousin Min claimed that years of working nights in show business had permanently altered her gastronomical clock. And for her entire stay with us, Ruby and I had to camp out on Grandmother's floor—a situation which Grandmother did not take to graciously. She complained that we snored, passed wind, exuded heat. In the middle of the night, she'd prod me awake to open the window. "How can anyone sleep with you two breathing up all the air?" she'd say. Only Ruby, who was just eight and didn't know enough not to, seemed to be having a good time.

Meanwhile, Cousin Min's trunk remained where Father had abandoned it at the bottom of the staircase in the hall. For days it sat there, a repository of mysteries, blocking the way to the second floor. Whenever I passed, I could not help touching the gold locks or running a hand along its gleaming black surface, and several times, I caught Ruby sitting on the stairs, gazing down at it.

Then, one afternoon, Min accompanied Mother and Grandmother to a Ladies Auxiliary meeting in town. Father was still at work, and Ruby and I had the house to ourselves.

"Come on, Myra," she called from the living room, where she was waiting to help me fold newspapers. In those days, I still had a delivery route, and a lot of the girls at my high school teased me for that. They also poked fun at the errand and odd job business I was trying to get started and began calling me Odd Job after the character in the James Bond movie. I just told them he was even scarier in the book.

Back in elementary school, I skipped a few grades, so all those girls are older than me; some even have boyfriends with driver's licenses. But I want to go places where a boyfriend with a driver's license can't take me. I'm aiming for the Ivy League. I want to major in business and, someday, own my own company. When I leave here, no one's going to tell stories about me like I've heard all my life about Cousin Min.

"So, how do we know that this person who claims to be Min is really who she says she is?" I asked Ruby as we sat folding newspapers. I was trying to spook her.

"Because Grandmother said," Ruby answered. "And so did Mother. You heard them."

I said, "Then, how do we know that they were right? It's not as if anyone asked for an I.D. check."

"Well, because," Ruby said.

I went to the bookshelf and pulled out the family photo album. After flipping through the pages, I took the album over to her and pointed out a snapshot of the young Minerva in front of the Bachelor Palms. "Doesn't look a bit like you-know-who," I said.

"But it *is* her." Ruby sounded confident. "I've seen proof."

She was not making any sense, and it was beginning to irritate me. I asked, "What proof?"

She said, "Other pictures. Things. Things in her trunk." Her eyes widened, and she covered her mouth with her hand.

I put down the album and moved slowly toward her. "And how did you get your hands on those? What do you suppose *she* would do if she knew you were snooping?"

"I didn't snoop," Ruby protested. "Cousin Min showed me."

I grabbed for her, but she sidestepped and yelled, "Fold your own dumb newspapers." Then she dashed for the door, but this time I got her.

She began to squeal. I clapped my hand over her mouth, and we scuffled out into the hall. "I want you to show me," I said. "Show me those *things*."

Now we are kneeling before Cousin Min's trunk, and I order her to open it.

She reaches for the heavy brass locks. Snap! Snap! The sound echoes through the quiet house, and the smell of cedar wafts toward us.

"Look," Ruby says, showing me a narrow black cylinder that fits into the palm of her hand. She pulls at one end and the cylinder telescopes into a gold-tipped walking stick. Next, she holds up a black fabric disk, about the size of a dinner plate, and waves it to one side; it opens into an elegant silk top hat. She flourishes the hat and raps the walking stick smartly against the wooden floor. We both laugh.

There is the sound of clapping behind us, and Cousin Min comes down the stairs. "Just the thought of going to one of those hen parties gives me a headache," she says taking the hat and walking stick. "I used these in a production of 'Puttin' on the Ritz.'" Then she is on her knees beside me, unzipping a garment bag, and a cloud of feathers drifts out into the hall. As she drapes me with a white silk dress covered with ostrich plumes, she says, "Ginger wore this when we danced 'Cheek to Cheek.'"

I think, Who is she kidding?, but I feel giddy. I glance over at Ruby, who is already lost.

"You still aren't sure about me, are you, Myra?" Cousin Min says, then unrolls a poster with a huge, color photograph on the front. It is unmistakably her, and she is dressed in black tie and tails. The words MI HO MIN NIGHTLY are printed in large red letters above her head.

She says, "In those days, I could do all of Fred's moves and, some said, better. He was a class act, but so was I. Everyone knew he shied away from flash, so I made sure I never did." She takes photo after photo from the trunk and lays them down in front of us. "Somersaults, backflips, handstands, the buck and wing. I did 'em all. Drove audiences crazy. Then in '52—or was it '54?—he came out with the ceiling dance in *Royal Wedding.* After that, all people wanted was camera tricks." Her voice has turned bitter.

"Tell us about the magic shoes," Ruby says.

Min looks up.

My sister reaches into the trunk and lifts out a pair of black and gold wingtips.

Min takes them, then says, "Sinbad had these custom-made at his uncle's factory in Hong Kong. He told me that as long as I wore them, I could give Astaire a run for his money." She turns the pair over and points to a row of Chinese characters inscribed on each instep. "They say, 'Good Fortune Dance.' Those words were branded on every shoe." She sits quietly, staring off for a while, then removes one of her house slippers and takes off her sock. "But here is something even Sinbad never knew about." Her voice is a whisper, drawing us close. On the sole of her foot, the words "Good Fortune Dance" have been tattooed in blue.

The next day was Saturday, and I'd spent the morning organizing my new errand service, which I'd decided to call Odd Jobs by Odd Job. I'd lined up customers and arranged to take on a partner, a friend I'd started out with at elementary school, named Winston Lee. From the beginning, our partnership has worked like this: I bring in the business, and he gets it done. Since the whole thing was my idea in the first place, I take 60 percent of the profits, and he keeps the rest, plus tips. I was considering whether I could afford to quit my newspaper route when I walked into the kitchen and found Ruby eating tuna sandwiches with Cousin Min. It was the first time I'd ever seen Min up and about before afternoon.

"We made one for you," Ruby said. "But hurry up and finish it because we've got to catch the bus."

"I'm taking you to the movies," Min added. "They're showing *That's Entertainment* over at the Pagoda Theater."

She had caught me off guard. Since that business with the tattoos, I was not exactly eager to spend another afternoon with her.

"It's the middle of the day," Grandmother said, coming into the kitchen. She and Mother had just returned from doing the food shopping. "Whoever heard of going to the movies in the middle of the day?"

"Besides, I'm kind of busy," I said.

"But you've got to see this movie," Min said. "It includes all of Fred Astaire's most famous numbers. I'll treat."

Mother looked up from putting food away in the refrigerator. "Go on, Myra. You can't be too busy to turn down an offer like that." She went to her purse and handed me a dollar. "Here, the popcorn's on me."

Grandmother frowned. She was counting on me to resist, but the crisp new bill in my hand had weakened my resolve. "Really, Myra." She sounded disgusted. I hesitated, but Ruby was already running off to fetch her pocketbook and put on her shoes.

It takes an hour and a half by bus to get to the Pagoda Theater, which is in the resort across the bay. During the ride over, Cousin Min didn't say much—not that she was a great conversationalist, but you could almost feel the gloom thickening around her. Ruby, on the other hand, would not shut up. Between choruses of "A Hundred Bottles of Beer in the Wall," she gave me a minute-by-minute account of every "Leave It to Beaver" rerun she'd ever seen.

There was a line at the box office when we arrived. It was hot, and red dust blew off the road and stuck to our sweaty skins. The starch in Min's suit had wilted. There were stares and whispered remarks as we purchased our tickets, then pushed our way through the crowd in the lobby. I was ready to sit in the first row we came to, but Min insisted on getting closer to the screen, and I could feel people staring again as we made our way down to the front. After we'd settled into our seats, the worst part was over, and by the time the lights had dimmed, I was almost feeling my old self again. During the previews, Min bought the popcorn.

But once the movie got started, it was all I could do to keep my eyes open. First, there was some guy playing a ukulele to a bunch of chorus girls doing the Charleston Hula. Then, Jimmy Durante singing that song he always sings. Then, a lady tap dancing on a row of giant birthday cakes.

I must have dozed off because the next thing I knew, Ruby is nudging me awake, and Astaire is dancing up the walls and across the ceiling of some hotel room, singing, "You're all the world to me."

"Leave me alone," I snap, but she persists.

"Hey, Myra, *wake up.*" I look where she is pointing, at the stage in front of the movie screen, and there is Cousin Min leaping, and whirling, and tapping up a storm, with the gold tips of her shoes glittering and the picture flickering all around her. I close my eyes, and when I open them again, she is still up there. "We've got to make her stop," I say. But Ruby looks as if she is under some kind of spell, just like when we were going through Min's trunk the afternoon before.

The teenage boys behind us begin whistling and yelling. Others join them. Some people throw things. Finally, the manager comes down and escorts us from the auditorium. He hands Ruby and me a couple of Three Musketeers bars from the concession stand on our way out. I almost throw mine into a trash can in front of the theater, but then I slip it into my pocket instead. Ruby opens hers right away. "Piggy," I say, reaching toward her, but she skips right past and falls into step beside Cousin Min. Then I notice that Min is humming. Her shoes make a clicking sound against the concrete sidewalk and the gold on them flashes as we head for the bus.

After that day, Ruby went tap dancing crazy. You could hear her upstairs in our bedroom, stomping away for hours while Cousin Min yelled instructions over the phonograph and the dishes rattled in the kitchen cupboards. Grandmother began spending most of her time visiting around the neighborhood. Then, one afternoon when I came home from school, the house was quiet. For a minute I thought Ruby had finally come to her senses and things had returned to normal, till I went into the kitchen where she and Min were talking to Mother.

"Guess what!" Ruby cried. Her face had the flushed look it always has when she is getting ready to spill the beans.

"Now, Ruby," Mother said. "This is Minerva's news; don't you think you should let her tell it?"

I didn't like the sound of that.

Mother opened a cardboard bakery box on the table and offered me a slice of chocolate cake.

"What news?" I asked, accepting a large corner piece.

Min smiled. "These last few weeks working with Ruby have made me realize how much I miss my old dancing days."

I began feeling hopeful and said, "You're not leaving, are you?"

"No, silly." Ruby could no longer contain herself. "She's going to open up her very own tap dancing school and stay here forever and ever."

"A what?" I said. "Where?"

"A tap dancing school," Min said. "At my daddy's old rooming house. Ruby and I checked it out this afternoon, and with a bit of renovation, the downstairs parlor would be perfect. There are even a couple of tenants still living there—Domingo Somebody and his wife Rafaela. Domingo is willing to lend a hand."

"But that's not the best part," Ruby said.

"Here, darling." Mother handed her a glass. "Go and get your sister some water."

Min continued. "In a couple of weeks, when we get the studio going, I'll move over to the rooming house, and Ruby can do all her practicing over there."

"Isn't that great, Myra?" Ruby said.

Grandmother pushed through the screen door and

came into the kitchen; she was home early. "What's great?" she asked.

"Cousin Min is starting her own dancing school," I said, relishing the prospect of getting my own room back, not to mention the peace and quiet.

"That's great all right," Grandmother said, pulling up a chair. "Just what the world needs. What's for dinner?"

"Come on, Grams," I said. "Why do you always have to be so negative?"

"I'm glad you feel that way," Mother said. "Because I've signed you up for lessons."

"Did you hear that, Myra?" Ruby cried.

I glared at her, then turned to our mother. "Well, I'm not going."

"What do you mean?" Ruby said.

I said, "I am not going to any *stupid* tap dancing lessons, that's what I mean."

"That sounds pretty negative to me," Grandmother said.

Cousin Min got up and left the room. Ruby began to whimper.

"See what you've done?" Mother snatched away my plate and stacked it with the rest of the dirty dishes. "I'm just asking for a little cooperation. Is that too much? All your life, I've done my best—"

My sister's crying grew louder.

"—cooking, cleaning . . ." Mother went on, clattering silverware.

"All right, I'll do it," I said. "Now, Ruby, shut up and don't go blabbing this to anyone."

She wiped her nose with the back of her hand, and nodded. Then she ran out to play in the yard. "Guess what!" I could hear her calling to one of the neighbors. "Myra and I are going to take *tap* dancing lessons!"

Cousin Min and Domingo gave the Palms a fresh coat of paint and installed a new floor, stage lights, and wall mirrors in the downstairs parlor. They acquired a termite-eaten piano and had it fumigated. Min framed her old publicity photos and hung them on the walls, and in a place of honor above the reception desk, she put up the color poster of herself.

But weeks passed when Ruby and I were the only students. I can't say I was surprised since that's what you get for not studying your market. Though I tried to point this out to Min, she had her own ideas; she'd already decided that business was suffering from a lack of publicity.

I thought of Grandmother drumming up the old ghost stories on her visits around town, then said, "You'd be surprised how word spreads in a small place like Luhi."

However, Min had had an inspiration, and it was this: she wanted to give Ruby and me free extra lessons in exchange for using us as advertising.

When I suggested that advertising is supposed to make people *want* to buy what you're selling, Min just said, "You've got to think positive. Remember, it's the positive thinkers who inherit the earth."

I was about to protest that wasn't how it went when I saw she was smiling. I told myself I felt sorry for her and couldn't quit then, but there was something in me that wanted to believe what she'd said.

The next thing I knew, Ruby and I were over at the studio three or four times a week, with supervised practice sessions in between. The extra lessons were supposed to help us improve more quickly, but neither of us was going anywhere fast. With her usual optimism, Min decided to sign us up for the annual Lions Club talent show at the county seat. "Remember, girls, think positive," she kept saying. This began to sound desperate as the date drew near.

There were twelve acts ahead of us; we were second to the last. By the time we came up, the auditorium was filled with the buzz of conversation, punctuated by outbreaks of coughing. Backstage, just before we were to go on, I peeked through the curtain at our mother and father in the front row. Grandmother had refused to come. Mother was trying not to look apprehensive, but she kept fidgeting with her hair. In the seat beside her, Father was asleep with his mouth open. "Come on, let's show 'em some real dancing," Min said, then walked out and took her place at the piano.

At the opening of "Tea for Two," Ruby and I enter— diggity, diggity, diggity. My legs are trembling so much it sounds as if I'm sneaking in extra taps. D-diggity d-diggity. "The beat," Ruby hisses at my back. For once there is a smart, self-confident sound to each step she takes. DIGgity. DIGgity. We launch into our shuffle. Doo wop shush. I think I hear Father snoring, but I can't be sure. Min is warbling, "Me for you and you for meeee."

Down in the front row, Mother is jabbing Father with her elbow, but his snoring gains volume, Khhhhhhhhhh. All over the auditorium, people are craning to see where the noise is coming from. I try to tap louder. DIGGITY. DIGGITY. DIGGITY. KKKKKHHHHHHHHHH, Father snores. Suddenly, the audience's attention shifts to something behind me. I listen for Ruby, but it is ominously quiet back there. "Three for two and we're for you," Cousin Min belts out. As casually as possible, I sneak a look. Ruby is untangling herself from the long extension cord attached to the microphone. I whip back around and try to focus on maintaining the pace, which seems to be accelerating with every bar. On the other side of the stage, Ruby has launched herself into fast forward and comes careening over to catch up with me. Diggitydiggitydiggitydiggity. "Ouch!" She kicks herself in the ankle and goes down. There is nothing circumspect about the laughter now. The next time I near stage left, I shuffle off into the wings. Everyone roars. I look for Ruby to follow me, but she has gotten back on her feet and continues dancing. She has a great big grin on her face.

After the Lions Club fiasco, I decided to cut my losses and hang up my tap shoes for good. Though Mother voiced some halfhearted protests, it was Ruby who saw my quitting as a major defection.

Meanwhile, Min had gotten permission from the head priest to move her operations to the abandoned Martial Arts Hall at the Buddhist temple. When I asked Ruby what was going on, she hinted that they were planning to out-Astaire Astaire, but refused to say more. I began passing the Hall on my way to and from school, just to keep an eye on things. Once I noticed Domingo unloading lengths of thick brown rope from a pickup. Often I'd hear the sound of hammering.

Then Ruby started having nightmares. One morning when she was dressing for school, I noticed a red streak, like a rash, around her middle.

"How'd you get that?" I asked.

She quickly slipped her dress over her head, and said, "It's nothing. You didn't see anything."

I began pulling her dress up. "You get this over at Min's?"

She shook her head.

"If you don't answer me this minute, I'm going to tell Ma," I said.

"I'll tell her you did it," she cried, and ran out the door.

That afternoon, I went over to the Hall right after school. The doors at the front of the building were locked, so I walked around back and let myself in through an unlatched window. It was dark inside—except for a spotlight shining down on what looked like a raised wooden platform. In the middle of the spot, a good fifteen feet above the ground, swung my sister.

"You've got to do better than that," a voice said. A second spot came on and there was Min, suspended from another rope right next to her. Min pantomimed a tap step. "How's the lighting from down there, Domingo?"

"Ruby, you come down from there this minute," I hollered. "You're scaring me to death."

Suddenly all the lights went on, and I could see that they were hanging from a weird system of ropes and pulleys held together by a metal scaffolding.

Ruby had stopped struggling and begun to wail. I ran over to Domingo and said, "You bring my sister down, or I'll call the cops!" But he was already lowering her.

"Myra, there's no need to excite yourself," Min called.

Domingo was undoing Ruby's harness. "You okay?" he asked. She had stopped crying.

"Come on, Rube, let's get out of here," I said. She

wouldn't come with me at first, so I grabbed her by the wrist and pulled her away.

Behind us, I could hear Min saying, "I don't think the ropes are going to do at all. We'll have to use cables."

Min decided to go ahead and launch her new act herself. She put up posters all over town advertising her opening night. "Air Tap, A New Concept in Motion," the posters said. For a whole week, she was the talk of the village. Every conversation began, "Did you hear what Kazuhiro's crazy girl is up to now?"

The show was scheduled to begin at eight o'clock. Min had borrowed extra chairs to accommodate the enormous opening night crowd, but at seven-thirty, Mother, Ruby, and I are the only ones there. At seven forty-five, the head priest shows up. It is so quiet, you can hear the mice squeaking in the walls.

Promptly at eight, the lights dim. A spotlight focuses on stage left. Dressed in black tails, Cousin Min enters to the recorded tune of "I Want to Be a Dancing Man." She soft-shoes up stage and down; right, then left. Each step is clean and precise. The tempo quickens. In spite of myself, I join in on the applause. She runs up one wall and backflips to a standing position. We applaud again. Next, she runs up the opposite wall and somersaults, but instead of landing, she sails right up into the air. We aah in unison. She performs a complicated sequence of tap steps and aerobatic maneuvers, accompanied by our nonstop clapping. Then, as she is coming out of a somersault, there is a sudden, terrible groan, the sound of twisting metal, and—*crash!*—Min flies through a wall of the set and disappears.

For an instant, we are too stunned to move. Domingo

comes reeling out from backstage. He is covered with plaster dust and there is a deep gash down the side of his face. "Call a doctor," he moans.

The priest is on his feet.

Someone is yelling, "Is she dead? Is she dead?"

"Shut up, Myra," Mother says. "Take care of your sister."

Ruby is white-faced and too shocked to cry, or even speak. We huddle next to each other as the priest goes to call an ambulance and Mother tends to Cousin Min.

Min was in surgery for nine hours. She had three broken ribs, a broken leg, a broken arm, a dislocated elbow, whiplash, a cracked hip, two slipped disks, a bruised spleen, a punctured lung, and a concussion. The doctor said she would probably never dance again.

Three times a week for as long as she was in the hospital, Ruby and Mother took her reading material and thermoses of seaweed soup. Mother occasionally bullied me into going too. Once, during the ride over, I read an article about Astaire in one of Ruby's movie magazines. The article told about all his most famous dancing stunts and how he'd pulled them off. It had pictures of "Puttin' on the Ritz," "Shoes with Wings On," and the ceiling dance from *Royal Wedding*. It even had a picture of the scene in *The Belle of New York* where he tap-danced in midair. I showed the photos to Ruby and mouthed the words, "Air Tap." When we arrived at the hospital, she left the magazine behind in the car.

.   .   .

After Min got out, Mother invited her to stay at our house until she was able to get around on her own. Ruby and I were given the job of helping with her physical therapy—a task I usually tried to avoid by pleading homework or a heavy lineup of Odd Job customers which Winston couldn't handle by himself. But one afternoon, Ruby was sick in bed with the flu and Mother wasn't around, so I had no choice but to pitch in.

"We almost showed up that Astaire, didn't we?" Min said, as I worked on her right leg, bending it at the knee, then straightening it.

"We came this close," she said. "Just wait till next time." I tried to shut out the sound of her voice by concentrating on what I was doing. Bending then straightening.

"Hey, Myra, what's it take to get two words out of you?" she persisted.

I stopped working on her leg, then looked her right in the face and said, "What do you mean next time? You were lucky there was someone around this time to scrape you off the floor."

She flinched just the slightest, then said, "I've had some bad luck. But that's never stopped me."

I said, "Well, it should. Anyway, what's the point? Even if Astaire knew you were alive, which he does not, there's nothing new about air dancing. He did it twenty years ago, in *The Belle of New York*. Without wires too." I got to my feet.

She was sitting on the floor with her legs sticking out in front of her. The tattoos on her soles looked blurred and faded. I realized they were not words at all but veins showing through her skin.

"Camera tricks!" she called after me, as I headed out of the room. "He did it with camera tricks." I knew she would never be able to get up by herself, but I kept right on going.

No one has seen Cousin Min since she's moved back into the Palms. Our mother continues to drop by, but Min refuses her visits.

Ruby has quit tap dancing and has decided to take over my paper route. One evening, as I am showing her where to make deliveries, we pass through Cousin Min's neighborhood. The windows of the rooming house are unlighted, except for the upstairs apartment where Domingo and Rafaela live.

"Hurry up," Ruby says. "It'll be dark soon. This place gives me the creeps at night."

"What's the matter, you worried about ghosts?" I tease.

She laughs nervously. "Maybe."

"Boy, you've sure changed your tune," I say.

Suddenly, she points over at the Palms. "Hey, Myra, look." The words are familiar. When I look where she is pointing, I see something white flitting against the sky. My heart gives a slight start, then I recognize Cousin Min lightly moving across the flat, concrete roof. She is dancing. I think I see the flash of gold on her feet.

"What's she doing up there?" I don't know what else to say. Min dances to the edge of the roof, and my amazement turns to dread. I step forward—to do what?—a shout caught in my throat.

But Ruby does not move.

Then, right before our very eyes, Min lifts her arms—a gesture from dreams of flight—and steps out onto the air. I wait for the plummet, the terrible thud, but it doesn't happen. The air holds her. She dances out above a huge plumeria tree, its white flowers glowing like stars in the gathering dusk. Then, she turns and lights upon the roof again.

"Did you catch *that?*" Ruby says. Her voice is breathless.

My eyes are still on the patch of white up on the roof. "Seeing's not always believing," I say.

The Bishop's Wife

Aki set the hair clippers on the vanity and examined her daughter's reflection in the mirror. "It's not stylish, but at least it's neat," she said.

According to the wall clock behind them, it was nearly noon. In a little over an hour, the Honolulu Bishop's wife would be flying in from the capital to interview the girl for the Buddhist Mission's annual college scholarship. It was the first time a high school senior from the village had been chosen as a finalist.

"Mama, I'm not at all sure about this," Missy began.

Before she could continue, Aki said, "It's too late now.

Didn't I tell you to go to Rosie? I'm sure she could have done a very professional job."

Rosie, the Barber Shop Lady's younger sister, had recently returned to Luhi with a diploma in hair science and had set up shop in her father's garage. Her specialty was in large hairdos. Even at a distance, you could not fail to spot her customers by their beehives and bouffants.

Missy did not point this out to her mother. Instead, she said, "I'm not talking about my hair. You could fix that easy by taking sixteen inches off the left side."

Aki picked up the hair clippers, then stepped back, frowning.

"Hey, I was just kidding," Missy said.

Aki was about to reprimand her for not treating the situation with the seriousness it deserved when she noticed the way Missy was gazing at herself in the mirror. She was wearing the moony look that had barely left her face since Koba Kobayashi first gave her a ride in his papa's fish truck a few months before.

"A few months, a few minutes," Aki muttered, rubbing her arthritic shoulder. "When you get old, everything aches."

Through the open window, she could hear her younger daughter Sachi calling to her rabbits in the yard and the tapping of her husband Makoto's chisel carving a name into a gravestone. A flock of mourning doves soared across the square of blue reflected in the mirror—wings flashing white, black, white in the sun.

She thought of Kitaro. His white teeth flashing in his laughing face. The way he'd turn one last time before disappearing into the breaking waves—with his spear gun and his empty net, the salty mist rising like steam around him.

That last summer, the sea had taken him from her every day.

As Aki looked into the glass, she could see the repeating shapes of time frozen in the reflection there. Her wide brow and stubborn mouth in Missy's dreaming face; her own face so much like her mother's photograph on the Buddhist altar next to the window. And outside the window, the slow life of the village—the hills and sea holding all the visible world like a single, perfectly contained thought.

Down in the yard, Makoto was singing a drinking song as he worked. Everything he sang became transformed into a dirge for carving gravestones. Now, the mournful cadence of the words blended with the sound of the chisel ringing against the stone: *"No-o-omuuu . . . nondeeee . . ."*

"Sit up straight," Aki snapped at Missy, then picked up a towel and began to brush the snippings from the girl's face and neck.

Missy straightened, but soon began to slouch again. Aki prodded her in the back. "Hey, jellyfish."

"Quit it, Mama," Missy protested and squirmed away.

Outside, the tapping had stopped, but the singing went on.

The old man would be finished carving that rock by now, Aki thought, if he hadn't sat in the yard all night, drinking with Koba's father. The stone was a rush order by Emigdio Manlapit, the foreman of Chicken Fight Camp. He was remarrying in the morning and wanted a high-class granite marker as a peace offering to his dead wife.

Aki herself didn't put much store in an afterlife, so it wasn't strictly out of religious feeling that she'd gone to

burn incense at the temple every day since Missy had entered the scholarship contest. But a person could use all the
luck she could get, and it didn't pay to be prejudiced about
where it came from. Aki thought, We'll go on doing just
fine too, if we can get a little cooperation from other people. She went to the window and called down to her husband, "Don't forget we have guests coming at one o'clock."

"I'm almost finished. Besides, there's plenty of time,"
Makoto answered, then returned to polishing his stone.

"And you, Miss Dirtyface," she called to Sachi, who
was standing by the hutch, feeding lettuce to her rabbits.
"Where did you get those greens?"

"Don't worry, Mama, it was just some old stuff lying
around the refrigerator," Sachi said.

"I worry that someone's going to get a good paddling if
I find out those rodents ate all the lettuce for the party
sandwiches. Get in here. Now!"

Aki pulled the window closed, then returned to the
vanity and began running a brush through Missy's hair.
She felt soothed by the coolness flowing through her hands
and the scratchy, rhythmic sound of the bristles. The scent
of lemon grass rose from the girl's damp scalp. It had taken
three shampooings just to wash out the ocean's smell.

Missy said, "Papa's right, you know."

"About what?" Aki asked, keeping her tone noncom-
mittal.

Missy said, "When he says that none of this matters all
that much." Sensing danger, she added, "I mean, it matters
a lot, but it doesn't, you know?"

"What is that supposed to mean?" Aki demanded. "Either it matters or it doesn't."

Downstairs, Makoto had come into the house and was
foraging in the kitchen. He was probably looking for his

store teeth. No telling where they'd turn up next—in the gardening shed, on a shelf in the refrigerator, among the tools on his workbench. She sighed. "You'd think a person could keep their own teeth in their own mouth," she said.

"But, Mama, I'm trying to tell you something," Missy objected.

Aki stopped brushing and looked up at the girl's reflection in the mirror. "I'm listening," she said.

Missy's gaze skittered about the room until it fastened on the new going-out dress hanging on the ironing rack. Aki looked at it too. She had spent hours poring over the Sears Roebuck catalogue before making her choice. The dress was made of pink voile and had puffed sleeves and a ruffled skirt with tiny red roses embroidered around the hem.

"So, something's wrong with the dress now?" Aki said.

Missy looked down at her hands and said, "Not exactly. It's just that it's . . . it's . . ."

"Sit up," Aki said.

Missy struggled on. "It's just that it's so . . . fancy! And so *pink*. You know how pink shows the dirt."

"Don't worry about the dirt. Just remember to sit up straight and you'll be fine."

Aki swept up the last of the hair clippings and headed for the door. She still had to arrange a relish tray like the one she'd seen in last week's issue of *Family Circle,* fix the sandwiches, and mix the lemonade. As she stepped into the hall, she turned and said, "Remember we've only got half an hour, so we can't be wasting any time. . . . Oh, what is that man doing now?"

It was unmistakable. From the kitchen came the smell of frying fish. Sachi called up the stairs, "Papa has his teeth, and he wants to know if you're hungry for lunch."

. . .

Aki removed the bedspread that protected the sofa uphol-
stery from everyday wear and raised the last of the living-
room windows. There was nothing she could do about the
smell, except hope that the Bishop's wife would be late.
Down the hill, the Kobayashi fish truck was parked next to
the Koyama Store. She could see Koba's muscular back,
bending and straightening, as he handed crates down to his
father.

She would miss his face around the house, but she'd
had to steel herself against him, for Missy's sake. She
thought again of Kitaro.

At first her mother had been proud. "My daughter is
engaged to the head priest's son," Aki would hear her telling friends. Then the questions had begun. Didn't he plan
on going to college? Did he expect to fritter his life away
on the beach? Where was his sense of family pride? Her
mother did not see, and Aki could not explain, that Kitaro
did not care about the other worlds promised in books and
prayers. The world he wanted was everywhere around him
—in the village, the hills, the sea.

"Do you want to spend your whole life buried in this
place?" her mother had demanded as the tiny world of the
village, with its network of obligations and personal histo-
ries, gathered Aki in with the boy's embrace. She had
breathed in its smell with the smell of salt that clung to his
hair, his skin. She had tasted its taste in his mouth, on
hers.

Then, one day, she had walked him down to the water,
and he had not returned. His body was never found. Grad-
ually, as she'd come to understand that she would not get
him back, the world he'd loved had narrowed around her,

drawing closer and closer until it covered her over, like the sea.

"Mama," her younger daughter was calling from the top of the stairs. "Missy is crying and won't come down!"

Aki sighed. There was still this to be done. When she walked into Missy's room, the girl was sitting on the edge of the bed, blowing her nose. Her hair was matted in streaks across her forehead, and the new going-out dress lay crumpled about her ankles. She looked up; they were too far apart to touch or speak. Once again, Aki could hear her mother shouting. Missy opened her mouth.

"No!" Aki cried and ran to her. She began pulling the dress over the girl's hips. "What will people think if you give up now?"

Missy stumbled to her feet. She moved clumsily, like a child confused by sleep, but she did not struggle.

"Hurry," Aki said, then picked up a brush and began smoothing Missy's hair. She remembered the strength in her mother's fingers, gripping her wrist, as they'd stumbled to the priest's house in the rain. It had rained as if it would never stop—the warm drops soaking the thin fabric of Aki's dress and revealing the fullness of her breasts, the ripe curve of her belly. She remembered how her mother had banged on the priest's front door. "Come out and look," her mother had shouted. "Look at what your son has done."

Missy twisted free. "No, Mama!" she cried, grabbing the brush and hurling it at the vanity. There was the sound of glass breaking, then all the brightness in the room seemed to go out.

The clock ticked. Out of habit, Aki glanced toward the

mirror, looking for the time. Jagged pieces of glass jutted out from around the great hole at the center of the frame. She reached up to touch her face, as if she would not find it there.

Missy walked to the closet and began pulling on a pair of jeans and a shirt. "Koba is waiting," she said. But her voice shook, and she would not look at her mother seated on the bed.

Aki closed her eyes, gathering herself.

When she finished dressing, Missy came to her, suddenly warm, suddenly hers again. "Please, Mama, let's not be mad anymore," she said.

Aki leaned toward her and grabbed both her hands. "Then stay here and talk to the Bishop's wife," she said. "Going to college would give you a whole new life. A life you can't possibly imagine now."

Missy pulled away, then said, "What would you know about that?"

Aki's jaw tightened. Somewhere in the house, a door opened and closed. Missy stared down the hill at the truck parked next to the grocery. "Anyway, this isn't about Koba," she said.

Aki got to her feet. "Then what on earth have we been talking about? Take off those things and put on your dress. I've had enough of this foolishness."

"It's not foolishness," Missy said. "You make everything I want into nothing, with your bullying and bullying."

"All right, Miss Know-it-all, tell me just what it is you think you want." Aki crossed her arms. "Go on."

Missy looked down. "I want to be here," she said.

"But didn't you just say this isn't about *him?*"

Outside, Makoto had begun singing again.

"I mean about Koba," Aki said.

"Stop it, Mama." Missy got to her feet. "I won't let you twist me all up so I forget what I'm thinking and if it's me or you who's thinking it." She looked out the window, at the dirt road running past the house. "You can want a place with your whole skin, the way you can want a person. It can fill your thoughts, without your even knowing; you only know that, if it wasn't there anymore, maybe you wouldn't have any thoughts at all."

Aki sat very still. It was happening again.

"Mama, that's what I want," Missy was saying.

The water was opening. . . .

Missy turned at the door and called, "Mama?"

When Aki looked up, she was no longer there.

Downstairs, the singsong of her younger daughter's voice drifted up from the yard. Probably fooling with those damn rabbits again. On the floor, the shattered pieces of mirror glittered in the sun. Numbly, she got to her feet and began sweeping them up. What would she tell the Bishop's wife? The fragments, clinking against the metal dustpan, reflected back the walls of the room, trapped sky from the window, a dozen tiny images of herself.

She heard Sachi calling and looked outside. The little girl pointed. "The Bishop Lady is coming!"

In the graveyard across the road, Aki saw Makoto in his blue suit, helping Emigdio set the new gravestone in place. Down the hill, a shiny black Buick trailed plumes of reddish dust as it made its way toward the house.

Talking to the Dead

We spoke of her in whispers as Aunty Talking to the Dead, the half-Hawaiian kahuna lady. But whenever there was a death in the village, she was the first to be sent for; the priest came second. For it was she who understood the wholeness of things—the significance of directions and colors. Prayers to appease the hungry ghosts. Elixirs for grief. Most times, she'd be out on her front porch, already waiting—her boy, Clinton, standing behind with her basket of spells—when the messenger arrived. People said she could smell a death from clear on the other side of the island, even as the dying person breathed his last. And if she fixed her eyes on you and named a day, you were already as good as six feet under.

I went to work as her apprentice when I was eighteen. That was in '48, the year Clinton graduated from mortician school on the GI bill. It was the talk for weeks—how he'd returned to open the Paradise Mortuary in the heart of the village and had brought the scientific spirit of free enterprise to the doorstep of the hereafter. I remember the advertisements for the Grand Opening, promising to modernize the funeral trade with Lifelike Artistic Techniques and Stringent Standards of Sanitation. The old woman, who had waited out the war for her son's return, stoically took his defection in stride and began looking for someone else to help out with her business.

At the time, I didn't have many prospects—more schooling didn't interest me, and my mother's attempts at marrying me off inevitably failed when I stood to shake hands with a prospective bridegroom and ended up towering a foot above him. "It would be bad enough if she just looked like a horse," I heard one of them complain, "but she's as big as one, too."

My mother dressed me in navy blue, on the theory that dark colors make things look less conspicuous. "Yuri, sit down," she'd hiss, tugging at my skirt as the decisive moment approached. I'd nod, sip my tea, smile through the introductions and small talk, till the time came for sealing the bargain with handshakes. Then, nothing on earth could keep me from getting to my feet. The go-between finally suggested that I consider taking up a trade. "After all, marriage isn't for everyone," she said. My mother said that that was a fact which remained to be proven, but meanwhile it wouldn't hurt if I took in sewing or learned to cut hair. I made up my mind to apprentice myself to Aunty Talking to the Dead.

The old woman's house was on the hill behind the village, just off the road to Chicken Fight Camp. She lived in an old plantation worker's bungalow with peeling green and white paint and a large, well-tended garden—mostly of flowering bushes and strong-smelling herbs.

"Aren't you a big one," a voice behind me said.

I started, then turned. It was the first time I had ever seen her up close.

"Hello, uh, Mrs. Dead," I stammered.

She was little, way under five feet, and wrinkled. Everything about her seemed the same color—her skin, her lips, her dress. Everything was just a slightly different shade of the same brown-gray, except her hair, which was absolutely white, and her tiny eyes, which glinted like metal. For a minute those eyes looked me up and down.

"Here," she said finally, thrusting an empty rice sack into my hands. "For collecting salt." Then she started down the road to the beach.

In the next few months we walked every inch of the hills and beaches around the village, and then some. I struggled behind, laden with strips of bark and leafy twigs, while Aunty marched three steps ahead, chanting. "This is *a'ali'i* to bring sleep—it must be dried in the shade on a hot day. This is *noni* for the heart, and *awa* for every kind of grief. This is *uhaloa* with the deep roots. If you are like that, death cannot easily take you."

"This is where you gather salt to preserve a corpse," I

hear her still. "This is where you cut to insert the salt." Her
words marked the places on my body, one by one.

That whole first year, not a day passed when I didn't
think of quitting. I tried to figure out a way of moving
back home without making it seem like I was admitting
anything.

"You know what people are saying, don't you?" my
mother said, lifting the lid of the bamboo steamer and setting a tray of freshly steamed meat buns on the already
crowded table before me. It was one of my few visits since
my apprenticeship, though I'd never been more than a couple of miles away, and she had stayed up the whole night
before, cooking. She'd prepared a canned ham with yellow
sweet potatoes, wing beans with pork, sweet and sour mustard cabbage, fresh raw yellowfin, pickled eggplant, and
rice with red beans. I had not seen so much food since the
night she tried to persuade Uncle Mongoose not to volun-
teer for the army. He went anyway, and on the last day of
training, just before he was to be shipped to Italy, he shot
himself in the head while cleaning his gun. "I always knew
that boy would come to no good," was all Mama said when
she heard the news.

"What do you mean you can't eat another bite?" she
fussed now. "Look at you, nothing but a bag of bones."

The truth was, there didn't seem to be much of a future
in my apprenticeship. In eleven and a half months I had
memorized most of the minor rituals of mourning and
learned to identify a couple of dozen herbs and all their
medicinal uses, but I had not seen, much less gotten to
practice on, a single honest-to-goodness corpse. "People live
longer these days," Aunty claimed.

But I knew it was because everyone, even from villages

across the bay, had begun taking their business to the Paradise Mortuary. The single event that had established Clinton's monopoly was the untimely death of old Mrs. Parmeter, the plantation owner's mother-in-law, who'd choked on a fishbone in the salmon mousse during a fund-raising luncheon for Famine Relief. Clinton had been chosen to be in charge of the funeral. After that, he'd taken to wearing three-piece suits, as a symbol of his new respectability, and was nominated as a Republican candidate for the village council.

"So, what are people saying?" I asked, finally pushing my plate away.

This was the cue that Mama had been waiting for. "They're saying that That Woman has gotten herself a pet donkey, though that's not the word they're using, of course." She paused dramatically; the implication was clear.

I began remembering things about living in my mother's house. The navy-blue dresses. The humiliating weekly tea ceremony lessons at the Buddhist temple.

"Give up this foolishness," she wheedled. "Mrs. Koyama tells me the Barber Shop Lady is looking for help."

"I think I'll stay right where I am," I said.

My mother fell silent. Then she jabbed a meat bun with her serving fork and lifted it onto my plate. "Here, have another helping," she said.

A few weeks later Aunty and I were called outside the village to perform a laying-out. It was early afternoon when Sheriff Kanoi came by to tell us that the body of Mustard Hayashi, the eldest of the Hayashi boys, had just been pulled from an irrigation ditch by a team of field workers.

He had apparently fallen in the night before, stone drunk, on his way home from the La Hula Rhumba Bar and Grill.

I began hurrying around, assembling Aunty's tools and potions, and checking that everything was in working order, but the old woman didn't turn a hair; she just sat calmly rocking back and forth and puffing on her skinny, long-stemmed pipe.

"Yuri, you stop that rattling around back there," she snapped, then turned to the sheriff. "My son Clinton could probably handle this. Why don't you ask him?"

Sheriff Kanoi hesitated before replying, "This looks like a tough case that's going to need some real expertise."

Aunty stopped rocking. "That's true, it was a bad death," she mused.

"Very bad," the sheriff agreed.

"The spirit is going to require some talking to," she continued. "You know, so it doesn't linger."

"And the family asked especially for you," he added.

No doubt because they didn't have any other choice, I thought. That morning, I'd run into Chinky Malloy, the assistant mortician at the Paradise, so I happened to know that Clinton was at a morticians' conference in Los Angeles and wouldn't be back for several days. But I didn't say a word.

When we arrived at the Hayashis', Mustard's body was lying on the green Formica table in the kitchen. It was the only room in the house with a door that faced north. Aunty claimed that a proper laying-out required a room with a north-facing door, so the spirit could find its way home to the land of the dead without getting lost.

Mustard's mother was leaning over his corpse, wailing, and her husband stood behind her, looking white-faced, and absently patting her on the back. The tiny kitchen was jammed with sobbing, nose-blowing mourners, and the air was thick with the smells of grief—perspiration, ladies' cologne, the previous night's cooking, and the faintest whiff of putrefying flesh. Aunty gripped me by the wrist and pushed her way to the front. The air pressed close, like someone's hot, wet breath on my face. My head reeled, and the room broke apart into dots of color. From far away I heard somebody say, "It's Aunty Talking to the Dead."

"Make room, make room," another voice called.

I looked down at Mustard, lying on the table in front of me, his eyes half open in that swollen, purple face. The smell was much stronger close up, and there were flies everywhere.

"We'll have to get rid of some of this bloat," Aunty said, thrusting a metal object into my hand.

People were leaving the room.

She went around to the other side of the table. "I'll start here," she said. "You work over there. Do just like I told you."

I nodded. This was the long-awaited moment. My moment. But it was already the beginning of the end. My knees buckled, and everything went dark.

Aunty performed the laying-out alone and never mentioned the episode again. But it was the talk of the village for weeks—how Yuri Shimabukuro, assistant to Aunty Talking to the Dead, passed out under the Hayashis' kitchen table and had to be tended by the grief-stricken mother of the dead boy.

My mother took to catching the bus to the plantation store three villages away whenever she needed to stock up on necessaries. "You're my daughter—how could I *not* be on your side?" was the way she put it, but the air buzzed with her unspoken recriminations. And whenever I went into the village, I was aware of the sly laughter behind my back, and Chinky Malloy smirking at me from behind the shutters of the Paradise Mortuary.

"She's giving the business a bad name," Clinton said, carefully removing his jacket and draping it across the back of the rickety wooden chair. He dusted the seat, looked at his hand with distaste before wiping it off on his handkerchief, then drew up the legs of his trousers, and sat.

Aunty retrieved her pipe from the smoking tray next to her rocker and filled the tiny brass bowl from a pouch of Bull Durham. "I'm glad you found time to drop by," she said. "You still going out with that skinny white girl?"

"You mean Marsha?" Clinton sounded defensive. "Sure, I see her sometimes. But I didn't come here to talk about that." He glanced over at where I was sitting on the sofa. "You think we could have some privacy?"

Aunty lit her pipe and puffed. "Yuri's my right-hand girl. Couldn't do without her."

"The Hayashis probably have their own opinion about that."

Aunty dismissed his insinuation with a wave of her hand. "There's no pleasing some people," she said. "Yuri's just young; she'll learn." She reached over and patted me on the knee, then looked him straight in the face. "Like we all did."

Clinton turned red. "Damn it, Mama," he sputtered, "this is no time to bring up the past. What counts is now, and right now your right-hand girl is turning you into a laughingstock!" His voice became soft, persuasive. "Look, you've worked hard all your life, and you deserve to retire. Now that my business is taking off, I can help you out. You know I'm only thinking about you."

"About the election to village council, you mean." I couldn't help it; the words just burst out of my mouth.

Aunty said, "You considering going into politics, son?"

"Mama, wake up!" Clinton hollered, like he'd wanted to all along. "You can talk to the dead till you're blue in the face, but *ain't no one listening*. The old ghosts have had it. You either get on the wheel of progress or you get run over."

For a long time after he left, Aunty sat in her rocking chair next to the window, rocking and smoking, without saying a word, just rocking and smoking, as the afternoon shadows spread beneath the trees and turned to night.

Then she began to sing—quietly, at first, but very sure. She sang the naming chants and the healing chants. She sang the stones, and trees, and stars back into their rightful places. Louder and louder she sang, making whole what had been broken.

Everything changed for me after Clinton's visit. I stopped going into the village and began spending all my time with Aunty Talking to the Dead. I followed her everywhere, carried her loads without complaint, memorized remedies, and mixed potions till my head spun and I went near blind. I wanted to know what *she* knew; I wanted to make what had happened at the Hayashis' go away. Not just in other people's minds. Not just because I'd become a laughing-stock, like Clinton said. But because I knew that I had to redeem myself for that one thing, or my moment—the sin-

gle instant of glory for which I had lived my entire life—
would be snatched beyond my reach forever.

Meanwhile, there were other layings-out. The
kitemaker who hanged himself. The crippled boy from
Chicken Fight Camp. The Vagrant. The Blindman. The
Blindman's dog.

"Do like I told you," Aunty would say before each one.
Then, "Give it time," when it was done.

But it was like living the same nightmare over and over
—just one look at a body and I was done for. For twenty-
five years, people in the village joked about my "indisposi-
tion." Last fall, my mother's funeral was held at the Paradise Mortuary. While the service was going on, I stood
outside on the cement walk for a long time, but I never
made it through the door. Little by little, I'd begun to give
up hope that my moment would ever arrive.

Then, a week ago, Aunty caught a chill, gathering *awa*
in the rain. The chill developed into a fever, and for the
first time since I'd known her, she took to her bed. I nursed
her with the remedies she'd taught me—sweat baths; euca-
lyptus steam; tea made from *ko'oko'olau*—but the fever
worsened. Her breathing became labored, and she grew
weaker. My few hours of sleep were filled with bad
dreams. Finally, aware of my betrayal, I walked to a house
up the road and telephoned for an ambulance.

"I'm sorry, Aunty," I kept saying, as the flashing red
light swept across the porch. The attendants had her on a
stretcher and were carrying her out the front door.

She reached up and grasped my arm, her grip still
strong. "You'll do okay, Yuri," the old woman whispered
hoarsely. "Clinton used to get so scared, he messed his
pants." She chuckled, then began to cough. One of the

attendants put an oxygen mask over her face. "Hush," he said. "There'll be plenty of time for talking later."

On the day of Aunty's wake, the entrance to the Paradise Mortuary was blocked. Workmen had dug up the front walk and carted the old concrete tiles away. They'd left a mound of gravel on the grass, stacked some bags of concrete next to it, and covered the bags with black tarps. There was an empty wheelbarrow parked to one side of the gravel mound. The entire front lawn had been roped off and a sign had been put up that said, "Please follow the arrows around to the back. We are making improvements in Paradise. The Management."

My stomach was beginning to play tricks, and I was feeling shaky. The old panic was mingled with an uneasiness which had not left me ever since I'd decided to call the ambulance. I kept thinking that it had been useless to call it since she'd gone and died anyway. Or maybe I had waited too long. I almost turned back, but I thought of what Aunty had told me about Clinton and pressed ahead. Numbly, I followed the two women in front of me.

"So, old Aunty Talking to the Dead has finally passed on," one of them, whom I recognized as Emi McAllister, said. She was with Pearlie Woo. Both were old classmates of mine.

I was having difficulty seeing—it was getting dark, and my head was spinning so.

"How old do you suppose she was?" Pearlie asked.

"Gosh, even when we were kids it seemed like she was at least a hundred," Emi said.

Pearlie laughed. " 'The Undead,' my brother used to call her."

"When we misbehaved," Emi said, "our mother always threatened to abandon us on the hill where Aunty lived. Mama would be beating us with a wooden spoon and hollering, 'This is gonna seem like nothing then.' "

Aunty had been laid out in a room near the center of the mortuary. The heavy, wine-colored drapes had been drawn across the windows and all the wall lamps turned very low, so it was darker indoors than it had been outside. Pearlie and Emi moved off into the front row. I headed for the back.

There were about thirty of us at the viewing, mostly from the old days—those who had grown up on stories about Aunty, or who remembered her from before the Paradise Mortuary. People got up and began filing past the casket. For a moment I felt dizzy again, but I glanced over at Clinton, looking prosperous and self-assured, accepting condolences, and I got into line.

The room was air conditioned and smelled of floor disinfectant and roses. Soft music came from speakers mounted on the walls. I drew nearer and nearer to the casket. Now there were four people ahead. Now three. I looked down at my feet, and I thought I would faint.

Then Pearlie Woo shrieked, "Her eyes!" People behind me began to murmur. "What—whose eyes?" Emi demanded. Pearlie pointed to the body in the casket. Emi cried, "My God, they're open!"

My heart turned to ice.

"What?" voices behind me were asking. "What about her eyes?"

"She said they're open," someone said.

"Aunty Talking to the Dead's eyes are open," someone else said.

Now Clinton was hurrying over.

"That's because she's not dead," still another voice added.

Clinton looked into the coffin, and his face went white. He turned quickly around and waved to his assistants across the room.

"I've heard about cases like this," someone was saying. "It's because she's looking for someone."

"I've heard that too! The old woman is trying to tell us something."

I was the only one there who knew. Aunty was talking to *me*. I clasped my hands together, hard, but they wouldn't stop shaking.

People began leaving the line. Others pressed in, trying to get a better look at the body, but a couple of Clinton's assistants had stationed themselves in front of the coffin, preventing anyone from getting too close. They had shut the lid, and Chinky Malloy was directing people out of the room.

"I'd like to take this opportunity to thank you all for coming here this evening," Clinton was saying. "I hope you will join us at the reception down the hall."

While everyone was eating, I stole back into the parlor and quietly—ever so quietly—went up to the casket, lifted the lid, and looked in.

At first I thought they had switched bodies on me and exchanged Aunty for some powdered and painted old grandmother, all pink and white, in a pink dress, and clutching a white rose to her chest. But there they were. Open. Aunty's eyes staring up at me.

Then I knew. This was *it:* my moment had arrived.

Aunty Talking to the Dead had come awake to bear me witness.

I walked through the deserted front rooms of the mortuary and out the front door. It was night. I got the wheelbarrow, loaded it with one of the tarps covering the bags of cement, and wheeled it back to the room where Aunty was. It squeaked terribly, and I stopped often to make sure no one had heard. From the back of the building came the clink of glassware and the buzz of voices. I had to work quickly—people would be leaving soon.

But this was the hardest part. Small as she was, it was very hard to lift her out of the coffin. She was horribly heavy, and unyielding as a bag of cement. I finally got her out and wrapped her in the tarp. I loaded her in the tray of the wheelbarrow—most of her, anyway; there was nothing I could do about her feet sticking out the front end. Then I wheeled her out of the mortuary, across the village square, and up the road, home.

Now, in the dark, the old woman is singing.

I have washed her with my own hands and worked the salt into the hollows of her body. I have dressed her in white and laid her in flowers.

Aunty, here are the beads you like to wear. Your favorite cakes. A quilt to keep away the chill. Here is *noni* for the heart and *awa* for every kind of grief.

Down the road a dog howls, and the sound of hammering echoes through the still air. "Looks like a burying tomorrow," the sleepers murmur, turning in their warm beds.

I bind the sandals to her feet and put the torch to the pyre.

The sky turns to light. The smoke climbs. Her ashes scatter, filling the wind.

And she sings, she sings, she sings.

The Prayer Lady

In late summer, when the spirits of the dead returned to eat with the living and to walk under the sky again, the villagers in the Japanese plantation camp put food out for the hungry ghosts and celebrated their coming with dance. On the last night of the *bon* festival, as time drew near for the lantern procession to light the spirits down to the sea, the retired head priest woke from a dream of falling water and called his wife to dress him in his white silk laying-out kimono. It was nearly time for their boy, Kitaro, to come for him, he said.

Okusan hurried into the living room where her hus-

band lay upon the couch, ensconced among stacks of dog-
eared journals and rolls of rice paper covered with Chinese
characters. As she stood trying to catch the drips from the
spoon she'd been using to stir the red bean soup, now getting ruined on the stove, she stifled the impulse to inquire
if their dead son had been informed of this plan. Instead,
she said, "Wouldn't you feel better if you had something to
eat?"

"I would feel just fine if other people didn't stand
around making unnecessary observations," Sensei snapped.
"Now hurry, woman, we mustn't keep Kitaro waiting."

Okusan looked closely at his face for new symptoms of
the falling-down sickness. She wasn't sure exactly what she
was looking for; three different medical specialists had been
unable to name the first attack, which had come on suddenly during a meeting of the temple elders a few months
before. Her husband had been the only one among that
gathering to oppose the new head priest's latest revenue-
making scheme of importing a rock star from Japan to
appear at the following year's *bon* festival. "I built this temple with my own hands before you were even a smile in
your papa's sleep," he had begun to object when, as he later
told it, the room suddenly turned very light, and then darkness covered him over like a wave.

The fit passed quickly, but it had left him paralyzed in
both legs. Word had spread through the village that the old
priest had finally been defeated by progress. For Okusan,
who did not put much store in progress, and especially not
in medical science, her husband's fit had been an almost
magical event—like all the sudden things that happened in
a person's life. She wished that her mother, who had been
well versed in traditional lore, were alive to advise her. One
cure, Okusan recalled, required little more than a change of

name to restore a person's health—a treatment which the old man had predictably resisted. He had not proved any more cooperative in her more recent attempts to seek out other, more suitable methods.

"Ugh, chives," Sensei grimaced as his wife bent over him. Each week she smelled of the most recent curative she'd heard about on the "People Speak" radio show. Though she was afflicted with rheumatism, she wasn't averse to trying out remedies for liver spots, heartburn, memory loss, or any of the other ailments people called in about. There was the period when she'd been consuming a bulb of garlic every day; that had been worse than the chives. But he had liked the lemon grass. He closed his eyes, as if to shut out the memory of that clean, tart scent.

"Old man, why are you in such a hurry to leave me?" Okusan knelt beside the couch. How thin he'd become; he'd had no appetite for days. Despite her earlier annoyance, she had no doubt he possessed the determination to die out of sheer cantankerousness, and she did not know how to stop him doing it.

"Let's call the Prayer Lady," she found herself saying. "It can't hurt to try." Then, taking her husband's silence as a sign of encouragement, she hurried on. "Didn't Nobu Kobayashi, the fish vendor, go to the Prayer Lady for that heart condition the doctors swore would kill him inside a year, and here he is, fifteen years later, even better than new? And what about Minerva Sato? She would have died for sure after that bad fall if the Prayer Lady hadn't gone to the hospital every day and prayed and prayed. And remember, oh, remember, the time last year when Little Grandma Mukai sprained her hip?"

Sensei remembered. Among the villagers, it was rumored that the Prayer Lady could heal people just by touching them with her hands. As the story went, she had acquired her special powers one rainy summer afternoon when she was carrying out the trash. A sudden gust of wind had blown the torn page from a sutra book across a neighbor's yard into her hand, and as she held the page, the full meaning of the text had filled her mind in an infusion of light. From that moment on, she had possessed a special connection with the Dharma that gave her the power to heal with her touch. For years, Sensei had regarded her as a less than creditable rival for the loyalty of his congregation. Who knows, he thought, if it hadn't been for that old fake carrying on her services down the road, church attendance might have been higher. And if attendance had been higher, he might have had better luck in convincing his superiors to appoint a more like-minded successor to his post. The image of the barely pubescent rock star with the ducktail hairdo flooded his consciousness.

"Hmph," he said.

Okusan pressed ahead. "So many people say such good things, such encouraging things, about the Prayer Lady."

"Stop calling her that," Sensei cried. "That old crank! That garbage-can Buddha! You'll kill me with your silly notions before Kitaro even arrives." His wizened face had drawn taut, and his eyes were bright. "Are you going to help me get ready or aren't you?"

Momentarily chastened, Okusan left to assemble the change of clothes her husband required. From the carved wooden chest in their bedroom she collected a pair of straw sandals, a yellowing silk robe, and a brocade sash decorated with gold and silver cranes. Through the open window she could see the ring of lights encircling the temple yard, and the festival-goers congregated on benches around the musicians' platform. "Hot noodles! Hot dogs! Genuine good

luck charms!" She could hear the cries of the hawkers ply-
ing their trade among the crowd.

She turned to examine the framed snapshot of their son
on the nightstand next to the bed. The picture had been
taken the day he drowned, nearly eighteen years before. By
the time her husband and she had gotten the news it had
been too late even to call the Prayer Lady. Suddenly,
Okusan knew what she had to do. She gathered up her
husband's things and started down the hall. Though he
called to her, she didn't stop as she passed the entrance to
the living room, but went straight to the kitchen and
picked up the phone.

"It's about time," Sensei said when she reappeared a
few minutes later.

"The soup was burning," she explained. "Are you sure
you wouldn't care for some?"

Outside, the last tour bus rattled in from the resort
across the bay. The doors hissed open, spilling out a stream
of tourist voices that flowed away across the parking lot, in
the direction of the festivities. Sensei said, "That would be
Tanji in his papa's truck, bringing our boy home to us."
Tanji had been a friend of Kitaro's. They had both died in
the same fishing accident.

Okusan sighed. Old man, even if you live through this,
you'll drive everyone away with your crazy talk, and that'll
be the same as being dead, she thought. Across the temple
yard, the drums began to beat and the bamboo flute sang
out an invitation to the dance. *"Arya sa, korya sa,"* the singers chanted. Inside their darkened living room, Okusan
wrapped her husband in funeral silk the color of old photographs.

The dream seemed painted there, behind his eyes. Always the same dream. The sea. The boy. Brown limbs

flashing against the white sand. Hands reaching up to re-
lease the kite into the bright sky, like a prayer. "Oh, look!"
Sensei could hear his son cry out, as the luminous shape
soared overhead. Kitaro was the last of his children, the
only one not buried in the sandy earth of the temple grave-
yard.

Sensei had built the temple with the labor of his hands
—hauling stone, mixing mortar, and sawing wood until he
thought he'd never stand straight again. But as he raised
walls and hammered roof beams, his body had grown taut
and brown. His faith had become strong. And long after
he'd finished with the mortising, shingling, and painting,
the structure had continued to shape what he'd become.
Through its doors he'd entered the life of the community.
He'd presided over weddings, births, and funerals, and
mourned his stillborn children there. In the dream he'd
dreamed within those walls, even the loss of Kitaro had
been made bearable by the embrace of ritual which had
bound the living and the dead.

Now, as the old man went back into that dream,
Okusan finished dressing him. "There," she said, propping
him into a sitting position, with a book of sutras on his lap
and his legs stretched out. "How handsome you look." The
reflection from the reading lamp behind him glowed upon
his smooth, bald scalp.

Okusan went to the window and peeked through the
blinds. "Is Kitaro out there?" her husband called. "What
do you see?"

The dancers were circling the musicians' tower, the
sleeves of their summer kimonos fluttering in the night
breeze. Before she could answer, the sound of footsteps
crossed the porch and someone knocked at the screen door.
"Good evening," a cheerful voice called out. The door

pulled open, and the Prayer Lady was standing on the stoop, with the light from the festival lanterns burning in the darkness behind her. She was dressed in a plain cotton shift, printed with tiny star-shaped flowers, and her white hair was neatly pulled back into a bun. She carried a bag of passion fruit and a bunch of golden chrysanthemums in her hands. "Hello, Okusan," she said, passing the flowers and fruit along, but her attention was focused on the old priest installed in his funeral clothes upon the couch. When she spoke, her voice was solemn. "If I'd known it was this serious, I'd have come sooner to pay my respects."

Sensei glared at his wife.

"I'll go and get some tea," Okusan said and hastily removed herself.

The Prayer Lady hadn't taken her eyes off the old priest. She nodded approvingly. "I see you've dropped a couple of pounds. A person who wasn't informed of your condition might even say it suited you."

"Um," Sensei grunted.

"In fact, if I didn't know Okusan better, I'd be tempted to think she was prone to exaggeration. You're holding up remarkably well," the Prayer Lady said.

"Um," Sensei grunted again.

"But I see it depresses you to talk about it." She went from window to window, pulling up the blinds. The night filled the room. The music soared. "Ah, but it's splendid out, isn't it? Smell that sea air."

"I heard you were in a retirement home," Sensei hissed.

The Prayer Lady settled into an easy chair facing him. "The things people say. You wouldn't believe what I've heard about *you*—that you've finally gone and lost your grip, and that it was the best thing that happened when the new priest took over."

Sensei glowered. "A point of view that you could appreciate, I'm sure."

The Prayer Lady shrugged. "I've never claimed to know what's best." She leaned toward him confidentially. "I do know, however, that it takes a lot more than missing a few dinners to starve yourself to death."

The old priest had pushed aside his cushions and was sitting upright. His face was flushed. *"Oi!"* he yelled for his wife.

"In fact," the Prayer Lady continued, "didn't Gandhi once go on a hunger strike that lasted an entire year? But I expect he wasn't surrounded by all this temptation." She gestured at the coffee table, piled high with baskets of fruit, plates of sweets, and other get-well offerings brought by members of the congregation.

"Omae!" Sensei yelled louder.

"This is quite a spread," she observed, helping herself to a sliver of Haru Hanabusa's tofu pie. She opened a greeting card, attached to a dish of pink and white rice cakes, and read aloud, " 'With best wishes for your speedy recovery, from Emiko McAllister.' "

"Get out!" Sensei was shaking with rage. "Get out, get out!"

The Prayer Lady remained unruffled. She wiped the crumbs from her mouth, then said, "I'd keep that pie refrigerated if I were you." She picked up her handbag and went to the door. Just as she was about to let herself out, she turned and faced the priest again. "Oh, Sensei," she said; it was the first time she had used the term of respect. "Neither of us could have held back what is happening."

He looked up, surprised by the gentleness in her voice, but she was already gone.

"What's all the fuss?" Okusan asked, carrying in a lacquer tray laden with tea things.

The old man didn't answer. After sitting still for a very long time, he laboriously swung one leg and then the other onto the floor and got to his feet. He waved aside his wife's offer of help and unsteadily made his way across the living room and out the front door. The night was alive with stars and the sound and smell of the sea. Okusan watched from the porch steps as he slowly crossed the temple yard and followed the procession of lights down to the bay. *"Arya sa, koryaa,"* the singers chanted. "It has been so. It shall always be." The lanterns glowed on the dark water as the words faded, and there was only the hiss of the waves on the sand.

ABOUT THE AUTHOR

Sylvia Watanabe was born in Hawaii on the island of Maui. She is the recipient of a Japanese American Citizens League National Literary Award and a creative writing fellowship from the National Endowment for the Arts. In 1989 she coedited *Home to Stay,* an anthology of Asian American women's fiction, with Carol Bruchac of the Greenfield Review Press.

"I first began writing because I wanted to record a way of life which I loved and which seemed in danger of dying away—as the value of island real estate rose, tourism prospered, and the prospect of unlimited development loomed in our future. I wanted to tell how the Lahaina coast looked before it was covered with resorts, how the old-time fishermen went torching at night out on the reefs, and how the iron-rich earth of the canefields smelled in the afternoon sun. I wanted to save my parents' and grandparents' stories.

"While this nostalgic impulse continues to color my work, I have begun to realize that tradition is not the static thing I once imagined and that the act of writing re-creates even as it records. In my fiction, I like to explore the forces which bring individual human beings of different cultures together, and to imagine the private struggles which arise from such meetings."